They strolled through the softly lighted club grounds, his hand tight and warm in hers. The evening air was scented with flowers as Michael plucked a red hibiscus and shyly tucked it into Lisa's thick hair.

"Your hair looks so pretty blowing in the breeze. That's the first thing I noticed about you."

Lisa shivered with a sensation she had never felt before.

"You cold? Here." He removed his baseball sweater and tied it around her neck by its sleeves. She put her head on his shoulder and they continued their quiet, dreamy walk along the fragrant path.

Lisa hoped she'd never wake up. . . .

Dear Readers,

We at Silhouette would like to thank all our readers for your many enthusiastic letters. In direct response to your encouragement, we are now publishing *four* FIRST LOVEs every month.

As always FIRST LOVEs are written especially for and about you—your hopes, your dreams, your ambitions.

Please continue to share your suggestions and comments with us; they play an important part in our pleasing you.

I invite you to write to us at the address below:

Nancy Jackson
Senior Editor
Silhouette Books
P.O. Box 769
New York, N.Y. 10019

DREAM LOVER
Constance Treadwell

First Love from Silhouette

Published by Silhouette Books New York

America's Publisher of Contemporary Romance

SILHOUETTE BOOKS, a Division of Simon & Schuster, Inc.
1230 Avenue of the Americas, New York, N.Y. 10020

ISBN: 0-671-53324-X

First Silhouette Books printing July, 1982

10 9 8 7 6 5 4

For Paul—my favorite Skipper

1

That's what I feel like—a fish out of water," said Lisa Harwood to her companion.

She knew that Michael Montgomery had been watching her long ebony hair blow in the stiff breeze. Now, as she spoke, he turned his blond head and squinted at the flying fish that were scooting over the vast expanse of water surrounding their boat.

"Wow," he said, "that's heavy. You're supposed to be on vacation, not figuring out your life."

"Yeah," Lisa said. She sighed—a sadder sigh than any fifteen-year-old girl should have to sigh.

The couple was sprawled on the deck of a sleek sailboat, named *Dream Weaver*, that was slicing through the navy-blue waters of the Gulf Stream, heading from Florida to Grand Bahama Island.

Lisa moved her agile, slender body to the lee of the huge sail so that its shadow could shade her porcelain-white skin from the harsh sun. Although she hardly knew Michael, Lisa was conscious of the warm glow that went through her as she watched him wriggle his supple form further into the brilliant sunlight.

She felt frumpy in her modest bathing suit. She wished she'd bought a sexier one—the one her mother had talked her out of.

"You wanted to make this trip on our boat, didn't you?" asked Michael.

"Oh, yes! When my dad asked how we should spend our month together, I told him I just wanted to go sailing." She propped an elbow on her boat cushion, pushed her huge sunglasses over her forehead and raised up to look at Michael's tanned and handsome face. "I was really thrilled when your dad invited us to go to the Bahamas with both of you on this fabulous boat."

"Do you only get to spend part of May and June with your father? You stay with your mother the rest of the time?"

"Yeah, I live in New Hampshire with my mom—she teaches at Dexter Academy. Dad lives in Boston. But it's such a hassle keeping up with the rest of the sophomores at Dexter that I don't get to see him very much. And my dad is the travelingest lawyer you ever saw."

"Don't tell me about traveling lawyers," said Michael. "I've lived with my pop for fifteen years, since I was two, and this month'll be the first time we've ever spent thirty days in a row together. He said this was my graduation present—I just got out of Broward High the other day." He gestured with his left hand so that Lisa couldn't miss the flash of his gold ring set with a sparkling sapphire.

"Congratulations! And let me see your class ring—it's terrific."

"Anyhow, it's super that our fathers are old friends and that they rigged up this trip. Pop gets a kick out of showing off his boat."

"Don't you stay with your mother at all?" Lisa asked him.

"Nope. When they split, they really split. She got married again. I think they have children, but I don't know for sure. Anyhow, I've never met any of 'em."

"Oh, how awful. Your own relatives."

"Yeah, well, she sends me birthday cards with mushy notes, but I haven't seen her in more than ten years. Her name's Margaret—would you believe I don't even remember her last name? She lives down south somewhere."

"Gosh," Lisa said, "that's rough. Still, it might be better than the mess I'm in—trying to be daddy's big girl and mommy's little girl." Lisa's tone was bitter.

"I don't know what you mean."

"I mean, my dad wants me to be Brooke Shields and my mom wants me to be Alice in Wonderland."

"Well, who do *you* want to be?"

"I'm too mixed up to know that." She heaved another great sigh. "That's why I said I felt like a fish out of water."

Suddenly the sails began slapping the wind noisily.

"Hey, up there," came a male voice from the cockpit, "the wind has shifted again. Someone go forward and help the big jib go across as I tack."

Lisa bounded to the bow of the boat and pulled a crease out of the large white sail and untangled the sheets. With these ropes loosened, the sail snapped to the opposite side. The boat heeled to a steep angle and Lisa carefully walked up the tilted side, holding on to the lifeline, sure that her Top-Siders would keep her feet firmly gripped to the slanting deck.

"You did that like a pro," Michael said as Lisa returned to her cushion. "When you said you liked sailing, I didn't realize you meant you knew how to sail."

"That's one of the few things I do well," she said. "When we were still a family we lived in Boston and I learned how to sail a small dinghy at the yacht club."

"That's how I learned, too," said Michael.

"That was fun. What was more fun was when I was about ten, dad got a twenty-nine-foot boat and took me out on it a lot. Mom was terrified of the water, and she really got mad when dad taught me to sail the big boat."

"I'll bet he did a good job," Michael said. "Hey, *Dream Weaver*'s dink can be rigged for sail. We'll have fun fooling around in it when we're anchored in the Islands."

"That'll be great," she said. "So, anyhow, a couple of years ago, right before the divorce I guess it was, I was out with dad and we got caught in a terrible storm. I was trying to reef the mainsail and I fell overboard. I was wearing a life vest and dad threw me a life ring and I got back aboard okay—except for an awful sprained ankle."

"What a trip! How'd your mom take that?"

"We never should've told her, she was furious! She raised a terrible fuss and kept on and on about it for so long that poor dad finally

11

sold the boat." She pushed her glasses up further on her nose and looked earnestly at Michael. "You know, I've always felt it was my fault that he had to do that. I still feel guilty about it."

"Aw, you shouldn't feel that way." Her despondent tone made Michael slip a friendly arm around Lisa's shoulders. She shivered at the unaccustomed thrill that pulsed through her body. She leaned her head against his chest and luxuriated in his comforting reassurances.

"Lisa, Michael, please come back to the cockpit, quickly."

"What's up, Pop?" Michael asked *Dream Weaver*'s Skipper.

"There's a stinkpot overtaking us. Get on the radio and see if you can raise her. Find out who she is, where she's going. Hurry."

Lisa's dad was watching the approaching powerboat through binoculars. Michael's dad was trimming the sails to urge a little more speed from his boat.

The Fathers, Lisa thought, I wonder why they're so excited about another boat sharing all this water.

The Skipper must have read her mind. He explained about boat hijackings that had been reported in Bahamian waters.

"What would they want from us?" Lisa asked.

"They're mostly drug smugglers, dangerous boat thieves who sometimes kill . . . don't look so frightened, Lisa. I've got two guns aboard in case of trouble. And I'm not looking for trouble, just making sure there won't be any."

Lisa heard a lot of crackling on the VHF radio. She heard Michael saying, "This is the sailing yacht *Dream Weaver* calling any vessel that can hear me. Come in please."

Then she heard a sultry female voice say, "This is *Happy Daze,* a houseboat out of Miami; we're right behind you. Do you read me, *Dream Weaver?*"

"I read you loud and clear," Michael answered.

"Where y'all headed?" drawled the voice.

"West End. And you?"

"Same place. Where are you from?"

"Fort Lauderdale—"

"Michael," said the Skipper, "you know better than to chatter on the radio. The boat seems okay. Sign off now."

Lisa sensed that Michael was embarrassed by the reprimand and she felt sorry for him.

She pushed her glasses into place and took a good look at The Fathers. There they were:

Skipper Bill Montgomery and his friend, John Harwood. Two successful lawyers, two bachelor parents. Two good-looking, carefree men looking forward to a month of fun. At least they'll be too busy to get in our hair, thought Lisa, as she daydreamed about the good times she and Michael had ahead of them.

"I know you'll think I'm dumb," Lisa said to The Fathers and Michael, "but I don't understand where we're going. You've talked about the Bahamas, Grand Bahama Island, the Islands, the Abacos, West End—you've really got me confused."

"Right now," the Skipper said, "we're heading northeast to Grand Bahama Island. West End is a large marina resort there. That's where we'll clear customs. Then we'll—"

"Hey, wait a minute," said Lisa. "How can we be heading northeast when the compass says we're going southeast?"

"That's confusing, I know. Our compass course *is* southeast, but the Gulf Stream is setting the boat north at about three miles an hour, so we have to allow for that."

"I thought this was the Atlantic Ocean. How do you know where the Gulf Stream is?"

"By the color. This dark blue water we're in now is very deep. When we get out of the Stream we'll be over the Bahama Banks in shallow water that's greenish blue."

"But I still don't understand. How can you plot a course that'll get us where we're going when all you go by is the color of the water?"

"I plot what's called a vector course. It uses our speed, the distance we have to go and the average three-mile set of the Stream."

"Sounds like a geometry problem," Lisa said.

"That's just what it is," said her dad. "You'll have to be our navigator, Lisa. You're the great mathematician in the family."

"You like *math*, Lisa?" asked Michael.

"It's my favorite subject. I think I'm going to major in it when I finally get to college."

"You *think*?" asked her dad. "I thought you'd already decided on that."

"Yeah, well, mom thinks I should be a writer of some sort. She keeps bugging me to major in English."

"Lisa," said her dad, "make up your own mind. Don't let your mother make such an important decision for you—she'll run your whole life if you let her."

"Oh, Dad, let's not start on mother again," Lisa sighed.

"That's right, old Dad," said the Skipper. "Let's drop the family feud. Besides, I haven't finished my travel lecture."

"Sorry—go on," Lisa and her dad said in unison.

"There's not much more. From West End we go east to a group of islands called the Abacos. Then for a few weeks we'll sail from island to island—they're called Keys but spelled C-a-y-s."

The raucous blast of a boat horn stopped any further conversation. A large boxy houseboat came slowly toward the port side of *Dream Weaver*. The Fathers, Michael and Lisa moved to the left side of the cockpit and watched as *Happy Daze* idled alongside them.

Two girls and two boys were leaning over the rail calling out greetings.

"Which one do you suppose is the one with the sexy voice?" Michael whispered to Lisa.

"Hey, y'all, I'm Jessica. And this is Cindy and David and Peter, and that's my Aunt Anita and Uncle Ed's driving the boat."

"Hi, everybody," called Michael, looking enthusiastically at the group—especially at the girl named Jessica.

"Hi," said Lisa, not so enthusiastically.

Lisa judged the boys to be about seventeen. They were sunburned right to the edges of their Jantzen swim briefs. Cindy's hair was hidden under a kerchief, her body enveloped in a red shirt, so it was hard to guess her age.

Since Michael had just said "Wow" under his breath, Lisa shoved her slipping glasses back up her nose so she could get a clearer look at Jessica. "Wow is right," Lisa muttered.

Jessica had long blonde hair that she swished through the air like a horse's tail. Her round face was punctuated by the makeup on her huge blue eyes and full, heart-shaped lips. From the neck up, Jessica seemed about sixteen.

From the neck down was a different matter! Lisa noted that Jessica amply filled out the skimpy bikini. Her long, tanned legs ended with toenails painted to match her mouth and fingertips.

Lisa looked down at her own prissy one-piece flowered bathing suit with its little boy legs and its not-so-very-filled-out top. Lisa had a clean, healthy, well-scrubbed look about her. She considered her good features: the long black hair framing her smooth, white skin, pert little nose, huge dark eyes and eyelashes so long they looked fake.

Even so, Lisa knew that no way could she ever compete with the sophisticated Jessica.

After some more small talk from Jessica and her gang, *Happy Daze'* throttles were opened slowly, and the big boat plowed through the water on course to West End.

Michael was still waving good-bye to the group.

Lisa continued to glare at Jessica's plentiful figure as it receded into the distance.

She sighed as she noted that Michael continued to wave to Jessica.

When *Dream Weaver* reached West End Marina the Skipper began to curse. "That miserable houseboat's taking up so much space there's not enough room left for a row-boat," he fumed. He glared at Lisa and Michael as though it were their fault that *Happy Daze* had fouled up his plans for clearing customs before the office closed for the day.

"Can't we take one of the empty slips?" asked Lisa. She pointed to the empty spaces with docks alongside and large pilings for docking lines.

"We could, but with so many boats ahead of us, we'll have to wait till morning to go through customs."

"What's so awful about that?"

"Well, for one thing, no one can get off the boat except me until we clear customs. We have to hoist a yellow quarantine flag," the Skipper explained to Lisa, "and no one but the captain can leave the boat until the Bahamian flag goes up—after the customs men get through with us."

"Oh, I see," said Lisa. "The marinas in

Boston cost about fifty cents a foot—it's probably even more here. It'd be stupid to spend all that money to sit aboard and look at the other boats."

The Fathers both said that it wasn't the money, it was the inconvenience. Then they went into a huddle to decide what to do.

"Man," Michael said, "that's what I like—a nice practical girl who's considerate of a guy's wallet." He gave Lisa an approving glance.

Lisa had usually resented all her mother's lectures on practicality. But she was pleased that Michael approved of this trait in her.

The Fathers announced, "We're going to motor around the bend—very carefully, because it's shallow, grassy water. But there are a few spots deep enough for us to anchor facing the hotel. We'll have dinner aboard, turn in early and get to customs first thing in the morning. Those people take forever, so we might as well get into a slip and spend tomorrow and tomorrow night here."

"This is a fun place, Lisa," Michael said. "Lots of good shopping, great food. We can go dancing tomorrow night."

"Sounds great," said Lisa. She was almost ashamed of how much she wanted to be quarantined as long as possible—with no one allowed to get on or off the boat. It would give her time to make some brownie points with Michael before he was exposed to Jessica's charms again.

They anchored *Dream Weaver* in the shallow bay close enough to the imposing Jack Tar Hotel to hear splashes from the resort's swimming pool.

"What're we gonna do about chow?" asked Michael. "I'm starving."

"Do whatever you and Lisa want," his dad said. "You two are in charge of the galley tonight, and any night we eat aboard. We'll all be on our own for breakfasts and lunches. But you and Lisa are the chief cooks and bottle washers for dinners."

The Fathers retreated to the cockpit with a cool drink.

Lisa explored the cupboards and well-filled icebox.

"It won't be as much work as he made it sound," said Michael. "We had a caterer plan the menus and stock most of the stuff we'll need. Here's the list—just pick a meal and we'll get going on it."

"Let's make something simple, I'm exhausted."

"We don't have to do much more than shove something in the oven."

They emptied a frozen pouch of *boeuf bour-*

guignon into a serving bowl and put it into the oven, then fixed a crisp chef's salad and garlic bread. The thick, wine-seasoned beef stew smelled delicious as it bubbled in the rich gravy.

"What a boat!" said Lisa. "Microwave, stereo, TV, hot showers—how long is she?"

"Fifty-two feet."

"Gee, you'd think a boat that size would at least have a dishwasher. I love to cook, but I hate doin' dishes."

"Me, too. That's why we have disposable dishes and disposable almost everything else," said Michael as he set the table with heavy foam plates, plastic iced tea glasses and sterling silverware. "The only bad thing is getting rid of all this trash."

Personally, Lisa thought it was unpatriotic to waste all those disposables that were made from oil—well, from petroleum derivatives, as she'd been studying in her economics class. But she certainly wouldn't tell Michael about that!

"How do we throw it away? Surely not chuck it overboard?"

"We don't even throw an apple core overboard! Sometimes the water is so clear here you can read the date on a coin. It'll make you sick to see the junk people throw overboard."

"I guess pollution's a problem no matter where you go. Some people are so dumb," said Lisa.

"Yeah, well, not us. We fill up heavy trash bags and stow them in the engine room until we hit a town with a garbage dump. Of course, you know who The Fathers will have doing that job, don't you? 'The Fathers'—now you've got me doing it."

Lisa smiled. "Well, they're so much alike I don't know which one is saying what. It's like they're both saying it."

"They're going to have plenty to say if we don't feed them soon."

After everyone enjoyed the meal, Michael and Lisa straightened up the galley. The Fathers talked lawyer talk in the comfortable salon.

This is what it must be like to be married, Lisa thought as she touched elbows with Michael. I wouldn't mind doing dishes with him every night, she decided. Then, remembering the stormy scenes in her parents' marriage, she made sure her daydream included a husband like the blond-haired Michael instead of her dad. She adored her father, but she'd given a lot of thought to the divorce and sometimes she could understand why her folks couldn't make a go of it.

Mom is so serious, Lisa mused, and dad is

so fun loving. Maybe if they hadn't had me, things would have been different, she said to herself.

She could still hear her dad yelling, "Why don't you let the kid grow up? Make her get her nose out of her books and go out and have fun like other kids."

"But she isn't like other children," mom would shout back. "She's a sensitive, serious girl—not the frivolous playgirl you'd like her to be."

Now, Lisa wiped away the tears that came just from remembering some of the dreadful fights she'd overheard.

"Lisa? Lisa, what's wrong?" Michael asked. "You've been drying that bowl for five minutes."

"I'm okay, nothing's wrong."

"Well, you look like you're asleep standing up. Are you too tired to sit on deck and see the sights?"

"No, I'm not all that tired—I was just thinking about something. Let's go."

"Better get a sweater, it's chilly here at night," said Michael. "I'll find us some deck chairs."

"It's just like fairyland over there," said Lisa from her comfortable seat on deck. "And listen to that music."

Yellow lights winked from the hotel's windows. Palm trees were woven with Christmas bulbs. Colored spotlights beamed on lush tropical shrubbery. An overhead glare from the swimming pool was softened by the evening dew. An excursion boat, docked near the sandy shoreline, seemed outlined with twinkling stars. A combo at poolside played Calypso tempos that wafted over the water and murmured seductive tunes into Lisa and Michael's ears.

"Oh, it's so beautiful, it's unreal," said Lisa.

"Wait till you see it in daylight," said Michael, "it really is unreal. A lot of fake beauty for the tourists."

"Please, Michael, don't break the spell."

"You really are a dreamer, aren't you, Lisa," said Michael softly.

She pushed up her glasses and looked directly into his compassionate eyes. "I'm just so confused, Michael. I feel I'm always alone —and not like other kids my age. Sometimes it helps to just daydream about a happier life."

Lisa sighed as though her whole life had to be settled before she was even old enough to get a driver's license.

"What d'ya mean?"

"Well, you know—my parents getting a divorce, and the way they fight about me and all that . . ."

"You've got to find out where you're coming

from, Lisa, then your folks won't bug you so much."

"Oh, Michael, you seem to know me better than I know myself."

"You must know that they both love you and that both of 'em just want what they think is best for you. You're a math whiz, Lisa. You remember that the total is equal to the sum of all its parts?"

Lisa nodded.

"So, life is kinda like math. The parts are your mom, your dad and you. You've got to add them all together to get the total of you, and who you are."

She sighed softly wishing it were that easy.

"Michael," she said, "it's really weird that you don't know your mother. Don't you ever wonder about her?"

"Yeah, I do. I used to try to get pop to tell me about her and everytime I'd bring up the subject he'd say, 'Don't ever talk to me about that woman.' Once he even told me that as long as I lived with him and he supported me, I was forbidden to ever try to get in touch with my mother."

"How awful for you. I wonder what she could have done to make him hate her so much?"

"Beats me."

Michael held Lisa's hand lightly as they sat

in companionable silence. She was giddy with the delight of these peaceful moments. But there was no way she could stifle a big yawn— she just couldn't stay awake any longer.

Once in her bunk, however, she was so exhausted she couldn't fall asleep. She was stretched out on the large, thick foam berth, snuggled under crisp sheets, a cozy blanket and cushy pillows. She lay there comfortable and relaxed as she reviewed the day's events.

Lisa couldn't believe that twenty-four hours ago she hadn't even met Michael!

Last night at about ten o'clock she had been asleep in the Fort Lauderdale hotel where she and her dad had checked in after their flight from Boston. They had dined in the hotel and then had window-shopped in the lobby arcade.

"That outfit would look great on you, Lisa." He pointed to a mannequin clad in Gloria Vanderbilt hot-pink jeans with a matching Danskin scoop-neck leotard.

"Mmmm—I don't know. It's not exactly my style."

"I'll bet your mother picked out what you're wearing, didn't she?" He passed a critical eye over Lisa's beige velvet blazer, white round-collared blouse, pleated plaid skirt and penny loafers.

"She always goes shopping with me, but she never makes me buy anything I don't like."

"Oh, there's nothing wrong with what you're wearing—it's okay for school, I'm sure. But maybe it's time for you to change your image—get some clothes with a little zing to them. Come on, let's look around in here."

The outfit zinged all right, Lisa thought as she slipped her slender body into it.

"That looks great, Lisa. We'll take it. The pink is wonderful with your dark hair and eyes—it'll look even better when you get a little color on your face."

"Dad, you know I never tan—just burn and peel."

"Of course I know, and your pearly-white skin is very appealing—'appealing,' is that a pun?"

"Not a very good one, but I appreciate the compliment."

"What I meant was—when you put on some makeup."

"I don't use much makeup," she had said.

"We'll see." Her dad had smiled when he said that.

Now, in her comfortable bunk, trying to fall asleep, Lisa drowsily pictured the pink jeans hanging in the clotheslocker in her cabin. She imagined Michael seeing her in this outfit.

Maybe he'd say "wow" as he did when he saw Jessica's bikini. Yes, she decided, she was glad to know the new clothes were there—and so different from the rest of her wardrobe.

As she drifted off to sleep, Lisa heard echos of young laughter from across the water. She heard Jessica's voice calling out, "Good night, y'all."

2

Lisa distinctly remembered that the Skipper had said, "You're on your own for breakfast."

Why, then, was dad shaking her from sleep saying, "Lisa, Lisa, wake up. I need some help with the coffee."

She jumped out of her bunk fast because she knew what a growler dad was before his morning coffee. She went into the head next to her cabin and washed up in the little bathroom's stainless steel sink.

It's funny, she thought, as she pulled on her clothes, when they were still a family she never saw anything wrong with mom getting up extra early to get dad's coffee ready. Now,

Lisa was strongly tempted to tell him to fix his own coffee! Is some of the stuff Michael's been talking about sinking in already? she wondered. It's so fantastic having someone like him to talk to. She shivered in anticipation of the month ahead.

Lisa and her dad scrounged around the galley looking for coffee makings.

"You're going to see all those kids from *Happy Daze* today, Lisa. What're you going to wear?"

"Oh, what I have on, I guess. What difference does it make?"

"I just want you to have lots of fun on this trip, and I think you'd have more confidence in yourself if you dressed like the rest of 'em. 'Clothes make the man,' they say!"

"Oh, Dad," she said, "that's not very funny even if it is early in the morning. Anyhow, if you're thinking I should wear my new outfit, forget it. Michael says all we're going to do is look around the place and do some shopping."

They still hadn't found anything with which to make coffee, and Lisa knew her dad was really getting frantic when he started lecturing so early in the morning.

"Oh, Michael, am I glad to see you!" said Lisa. "Where's the coffee stuff?"

"Ooops, I should have shown you how we do it." He reached into the deep freeze and took an ice cube tray from a tall stack. He popped out two very black cubes and put each one in a heavy ceramic mug.

"Might as well make a cup for pop, too. He's a bear until he gets his morning fix."

Lisa and her dad watched in amazement as Michael filled the mugs with water and put them into the microwave. In less than two minutes the cabin was filled with the aroma of strong coffee.

"Neat," Lisa said. "You'll make someone a great husband, Michael."

The Skipper appeared in the galley and reached out a hand for his coffee mug. The Fathers sat at the dinette table in silence and slurped their brew.

"Lisa, did you see any peanut butter while you were poking around the galley?" asked Michael. "I got up in the middle of the night 'cause I was starving, but I couldn't find the peanut butter."

Lisa wished she'd heard him. She'd have gotten up, too, and they could've had a romantic midnight snack together.

"No peanut butter? How awful! That's all I ever eat for breakfast—a peanut butter sandwich and orange juice."

"I'm amazed that your mother doesn't make you eat oatmeal," her dad commented.

"Oh, Dad, please stop picking on mother."

"Do you mean to say, Michael," said his pop, "that you didn't tell the caterer you wanted peanut butter put aboard?"

"Oh, Pop, lay off, will ya?" Michael said. "That's a coincidence, Lisa. My usual breakfast is a peanut butter and banana sandwich and orange juice."

"That's a new one on me. I'll try it, as soon as we get some peanut butter." She thought how wonderful it was that they both liked the same things.

"We'll get some as soon as we go ashore. Now, let's see what we can dig up for breakfast."

He poked into the freezer again, found a frozen Danish coffeecake, put it on a paper plate and placed it in the microwave. He dumped some cocoa mix into mugs, added water and stuck the cups into the oven, too. The Fathers actually fixed their own second cups of black ice cubes—and liberally helped themselves to the Danish that was oozing with apricots and French crumbs.

Lisa giggled to herself at the thought of what her mom would have to say about this junk food breakfast.

By the time Lisa and Michael finished eating and making the galley and cabins shipshape, The Fathers had warmed up *Dream Weaver*'s engine, had weighed anchor and

were carefully maneuvering the boat alongside the customs dock—into a vacant slot
right in front of *Happy Daze.*

"Lisa," said the Skipper, "how about hoisting this yellow flag for me?"

"Can I have a few minutes to change
clothes?"

"Not now. The sooner the customs people
see the flag, the sooner they'll get to us."

"Maybe Michael could do it."

"I need Michael to help me get the ship's
papers together. And your dad is making
notes for a phone call he has to make when he
goes ashore. C'mon, Lisa, hop to it."

Lisa went topside and attached the quarantine flag to thin lines and hoisted the signal up
the halyard. As she looked upward to check
that it wasn't caught on any of the boat's
rigging, she caught a glimpse of the colorful
Bahamian courtesy flag fluttering from the
flagstaff on *Happy Daze.*

Jessica spotted Lisa and walked toward her.

"Hey, there," Jessica said. "It's . . . um . . .
Lisa, isn't it?"

"Yes—hi, Jessica."

"You're not through customs yet? We did it
yesterday. We had a fabulous time last night
dancing at the hotel. Then we went for a late
swim."

"Michael and I had a fabulous time, too. We sat on deck all evening looking at the lights on shore and . . . and just talking."

"By the way, where's Michael?" Jessica asked.

"Below—helping his pop."

And I hope he stays there till you leave, Lisa said to herself. She felt like such a nerd standing there alongside the sophisticated Jessica.

Jessica was poured into white jeans—so tight that the designer's logo looked as though it were stretched in embroidery hoops. She probably got into the shower with them, Lisa thought to herself, and let them dry while she was wearing them.

Lisa saw Jessica's three friends roaming around the docks, looking at the boats and talking to other young boat people. They looked like a flock of peacocks, she thought. The girls in their brilliantly colored jeans and splashy print tops; the boys in their Levis and vivid T-shirts. She noticed several crazy shirts with "It's Better in the Bahamas" across the front.

Right now, Lisa wasn't so sure of the truth of that slogan. She looked down at her navy-blue T-shirt that read "Sailors Have More Fun." She wasn't so sure about that, either. Her J. G. Hook chino slacks, so "in" at home, looked colorless and uninteresting in the bright sunshine.

Lisa wished she'd been allowed to take time to change into her hot-pink jeans. She couldn't wait for Michael to see that she could look as good as Jessica—well, almost.

"Is Michael your boyfriend?" asked Jessica.

"Well, I just met him yesterday, but we get along great. I . . . I like him a lot."

"Yeah, and there's a lot of him to like," said Jessica. Her big blue eyes brightened.

"How about you? Which of your crew—I don't remember their names—is your boyfriend?"

"Oh, neither of 'em. David and Peter are just kids my aunt and uncle asked along to keep Cindy and me company. Cindy's my best friend from home."

"I see," said Lisa. They aren't her boyfriends, she thought with dismay.

"The guys are the sons of friends of Aunt Anita and Uncle Ed. They're from Miami—just got out of high school. I'll be a senior, what're you?"

"Junior." said Lisa.

"How about Michael—what's he—how old is he?"

"Seventeen. Michael just grad—"

"Someone taking my name in vain?" said Michael as he came topside. His lips pursed into an appreciative, though silent, whistle when he saw Jessica draped over *Dream Weaver*'s lifelines.

"Hell-o-o-o, Jessica. How're y'all doin'?"

"Hey, there, Michael. I'll have to teach you to talk southern—you never say 'y'all' to one person."

"Sho' 'nuff, honey child! When do the lessons start?"

Lisa couldn't believe this was Michael. Her serious, understanding Michael, flirting like a sophomore with . . . with . . . Scarlett O'Hara —no, with Jezebel.

While Lisa swallowed the lump in her throat, two customs men arrived. They asked permission to board *Dream Weaver*. Michael and Lisa followed them into the cockpit. Jessica continued to stand alongside.

Michael's pop talked to the polite and businesslike inspectors. He produced the necessary papers and he had to declare the two guns that were aboard.

Just hearing about the weapons frightened Lisa—although she would like to aim one at Jessica, who was still standing there.

One of the officials asked in a clipped English accent if *Dream Weaver* carried any pets, exotic plants or drugs.

"Gee, aren't they even going to search

below?" Lisa whispered to Michael. "What kind of inspection is that?"

"I guess we don't look suspicious. Are you having any trouble filling out your form?"

When Michael said that, Jessica looked at Lisa's slight figure and gave a derisive hoot.

Lisa cringed and was thankful that Michael did not seem to have heard.

"What's this mean," Lisa asked, "proof of citizenship?"

"Driver's license, birth certificate, whatever you have to prove you're you."

"Oh, Michael, you're really robbing the cradle—Lisa isn't old enough to drive," Jessica interjected.

The Skipper sternly told Jessica to go away and let them finish their business with the customs men.

"Lisa," exploded her dad, "do you mean to say that your know-it-all mother didn't realize you'd need some proof of citizenship?"

"Why should she have known that? You're the one who ought to have told me I'd need my birth certificate."

Her dad raised an eyebrow at Lisa's rare display of temper. Michael gave her a reassuring pat on the arm. She was sure he wanted to let her know that he was on her side. Her mood brightened.

"Now, now, little lady, it's no matter," said the tall inspector in his cultured accent. "We won't be sticky about it. I'll just initial that paper and you're cleared—as welcome here as anyone else."

"Thank you very much," said Lisa, primly. She was awed by the courteous authority of the two officials. And she was angry at her father's outburst, and at Jessica's unkind thrusts. But mostly, she was hurt by Michael's flirtation with that southern siren.

"Everything's in order, Captain. Here are immigration cards for each of you. Please turn them in when you leave our country. We hope you will enjoy your visit here."

The Fathers lost no time in doing just that. They picked up their golf clubs and set off for eighteen holes of fun and exercise.

As Lisa's dad passed her, he slipped her some money and a credit card and said, "Here, Pet, go buy yourself some clothes as pretty as you are. And, don't forget, I love you very much."

"I'm having a peanut butter attack," said Michael. "C'mon, Lisa, let's get some food and sit on the beach and eat. Hurry, I'm starving."

"Just give me a minute to change my clothes."

"Why bother? You look okay."

Lisa looked at Michael's worn, faded jeans and his Lacoste shirt that used to be white but was now grey; now even the alligator had lost its color. She wondered how important clothes were to him. Her dad had just said that the way you dressed gave you confidence. But Michael was self-assured and she'd never seen him look any way but sloppy. Then she remembered Michael's reactions to Jessica, and she knew she'd have to test her dad's suggestion. Not that she wanted to dress like Jessica! But she wanted to get more response from Michael than just "you look okay."

"I'm glad they had crunchy," said Michael as they left the Mini-Supermarket. "I hate smooth."

"Ugh, crunchy takes too long to chew."

"So now we have his and hers jars of peanut butter," he said.

From nowhere, Lisa got a mental picture of her old home: mom's chair, dad's chair, mom's coffee cup, dad's coffee cup. She sighed and thought—so much for his and hers; now they couldn't even be polite to each other.

"Lisa, you're miles away again. Will you stop brooding and start enjoying yourself. Look, there's the pool we saw last night. Doesn't look like fairyland now, does it?"

"Nope, you were right, it's just another pool. And listen to the noise, everyone's yelling over the music. It's sure not as peaceful here as it seemed last night."

"You'll find plenty to dream about when you see some of the great places we're going. Hey, let's sit on the seawall and eat."

Michael looked down at the hand that held a banana and he let out an anguished squeal. "Oh, my gosh! My ring, my class ring, it's gone."

He held out his left hand and all that showed on his third finger was the unsuntanned outline of his large ring.

"Michael, how awful," said Lisa. "Oh, wait a minute! You took it off when you were washing the breakfast dishes. Don't you remember? You—"

"Oh, hey, that's right! I hung it on that magnet thing on the side of the oven. You know what I mean, that hook for the pot holders. What a relief! My pop would kill me if I lost that."

"Well, that's where it is, so don't worry about it."

"Wow, pop sure raised the roof when I ordered a real sapphire instead of a fake one. He told me I'd take the ring off as soon as I got to college, and I'd probably hock it for the dough to buy a fraternity pin—I'm going to FSU in Tallahassee, you know."

"Oh, yeah, I've heard of Florida State."

"Pop said I really wanted the fancy ring to wow the girls on the beach this summer."

"What'd he mean by that?"

"I'm gonna lifeguard at the Fort Lauderdale beach from July Fourth till Labor Day."

"That's cool! You know, we really have a lot in common. My summer job is at the same time—I'm gonna type a thesis for one of my professors."

"That sounds like hard work."

"It was all I could find. My mom thinks I should earn money for school stuff. Wish I had some jewelery to hock. At what this guy's going to pay me, I'll be lucky to afford a pair of loafers."

"Yeah, my pop thinks I should use my life-guarding money for school, too. Listen, Lisa, I've seen this place a dozen times, but why don't you walk around and see the sights. I've gotta shop for jeans and some other stuff—pop said I looked 'disreputable' in these."

Lisa pushed up her glasses with her usual unconscious gesture and gazed directly at Michael.

"I'd like to be alone for a while, okay? I'll just go back to the boat."

"Okay. I'll see you there in awhile."

Oh, boy, Lisa plotted to herself, this would be the perfect chance to make Michael really appreciate her. She'd get his ring from the galley, find him in one of the stores and give it to him. He'd be so happy to have that worry off his mind, she decided, that they'd go shopping together and she'd be alone with him all the rest of the day.

Just as she started along the palm-lined path to the boat, she heard Jessica call to Michael!

"Hey, Michael—where've you been? How about some tennis?"

"Sure, that'd be great. I'll meet you at the courts after I pick up my tennis stuff."

"Oh, I'll just come along with you and wait," Jessica said.

Hearing this, Lisa walked so quickly in the opposite direction she almost fell into a cactus plant. Jessica must have been waiting to catch Michael alone! Why should she let Jessica get away with such a sneaky trick? And she would get away with it if Lisa just stood there. She decided to go back to the boat as she'd planned and check out the action for herself.

Jessica was looking around the galley as Lisa got aboard *Dream Weaver*. "Jessica, what're you doing here?" asked Lisa innocently. "Where's Michael?"

"Here I am, Lisa," he called from the dinette. "I'm hunting my tennis racket—thought I'd stowed it under this seat. Where've you been? I was surprised you weren't aboard when Jessica and I got here."

"I'm surprised you're here—the rackets are under the other seat—I thought you were going shopping."

"I ran into Jessica and we decided to play tennis."

That's what you think, Lisa thought. Boy, but boys can be dumb.

"Come play with us," Michael continued. "We'll wait for you to change. Okay, Jessica?"

"I guess so—but maybe Lisa has something else planned."

"Nothing special," said Lisa. "I'll be ready in a few minutes. Michael, will ya get my racket, too?"

Michael followed Lisa to her cabin. "Lisa, can you hear me?"

"Yes, of course. What is it? What's the matter?"

"It's my ring! It's not there, I just can't find it!" he said in a frantic voice.

"Are you sure? Did you look all around the stove? Maybe it fell off the hook."

"I've looked everywhere in the galley. I just said I was looking for my racket when you came in, I was really searching around the dinette."

Lisa came out of the cabin. Michael was so worried about the disappearance of his ring that he didn't even look up to notice how cute she looked in her white tennis dress, her long hair tied in a ponytail.

"It must be around somewhere, Michael. Maybe the boat rocked and the ring fell on the carpet and rolled around."

"I've looked all over the carpet, it's just not here."

"Listen, you go play tennis with Jessica and I'll stay here and search some more."

"Oh, that's silly, Lisa. You're probably right —it rolled around the carpet and is hidden under something. We'll find it later. C'mon, Jessica will be wondering where we are."

They strolled three abreast toward the courts. When Lisa lagged behind to smear her white skin with suntan lotion, she heard Jessica say to Michael, "Why'd you have to drag her along with us?"

"Why not? She's a great kid."

"I'm sure she is," said Jessica. "Listen, Michael, I couldn't help overhearing the two of you talking about your ring. You know, *she* could have stolen it."

"Jessica, that's stupid! Why would Lisa take my ring?"

"Well, she's got an awful crush on you and—"

"What a dumb thing to say! Just forget it, Jessica. I'll find the thing later."

"But, Michael," Jessica persisted, "girls just love to get a boy's school ring. I know Lisa is crazy about you. She could've wanted your ring badly enough to steal it."

"Please, Jessica, let's drop it!"

"But you heard her tell you to go play tennis and she'd look for the ring. When she saw how shook up you were, she probably planned to just happen to find it."

"Jessica, that's crazy! Just shut up! Forget it!"

Lisa was stunned by what she had overheard. She was angry and upset. She realized she couldn't let them know she'd heard their conversation. All she wanted to do now was to run away and be somewhere by herself. She could barely force herself to rejoin Michael and Jessica.

"Listen," she said when she had caught up to them, "it's too hot for tennis. You two go on and play. I don't feel like it anymore. I think I'll just go back to the boat."

Lisa saw Jessica send Michael a "see, I told you so" look.

"Aw, c'mon and play a couple of sets, Lisa. We'll quit when it gets too hot," Michael said. "Gee you look great! I'll bet you're a fabulous player."

"Honest, I don't want to play."

"Michael," said Jessica, "let her go back to the boat if she wants to. Maybe she'll find your ring," she added significantly. She turned to Lisa and said, "I heard y'all talking about it, and I'm sure you'll find it for him."

"Please, Lisa, play for a little while," pleaded Michael.

Why didn't Michael want her to go back to *Dream Weaver*, Lisa wondered. She shuddered with the fear that he might be taking Jessica's charges seriously.

David, or was it Peter, Lisa wasn't sure which boy was which, seemed to be waiting for Jessica at the courts. He appeared surprised that two extra players had been added to the game.

"Girls against boys," shrilled Jessica. "Okay, David?"

The girls volleyed with Michael and David, but Lisa couldn't concentrate on the play. She was shocked and revolted by what was happening between her and Michael. They were such great pals—he seemed to like her as much as she liked him, Lisa thought. Surely he didn't, couldn't, wouldn't, believe Jessica?

Jessica was pirouetting on both sides of the doubles court.

Suddenly, anger overcame Lisa. She wanted to slam that little yellow ball with all her strength. She put every bit of her energy and rage into the volleys. All her fury was taken out on the taut nylon strings of her racket.

"Wow, you can really play when you want to," Michael called to Lisa.

"Yeah," said David, "you sure hit a mean ball!"

Jessica seemed to take these compliments to Lisa as criticisms of her own weak game. She continued to hog the court and take shots meant for Lisa.

A fast ball came across the net, down the middle line. It was a hard backhand shot for Jessica. It was an easy forehand return for Lisa. Jessica moved slightly to the left to take the ball. Lisa quickly moved to the right for the hit. Then the spinning ball took a bad bounce. Its power died and it rolled along the court, away from both girls.

But Lisa's right arm was still fully extended, the metal racket held rigid by her wrist and fingers. She automatically pulled her arm back, ready to give the ball a mighty sock. She completed her strong swing. And her racket hit Jessica's cute little backside.

3

"Lisa, what'd you do that for?" demanded Michael. He'd just returned to *Dream Weaver* and found Lisa on her knees in the galley.

"I'm looking for your ring. It must be around here somewhere."

"No, I mean, why'd you hit Jessica?"

"I didn't hit Jessica! She was out of position and got in the way of my racket. I couldn't help it. I couldn't stop my swing once I started."

"Yeah?"

"Yeah."

"Okay, if you say so, Lisa. Where'll I start looking?"

"The only place I haven't searched is the

cabin where The Fathers sleep. Do you think you could have left it there?"

"I wasn't even in there. And I *know* I hung it on the hook beside the oven."

"Aw, Michael, think again. Maybe you took it off the hook and put it down someplace else. Maybe in the head when you washed your hands, or on your bunk when you made it. Oh, I don't know, it could be anyplace."

"I've looked everywhere like that; *you've* looked all over. It's useless to keep hunting. Let's try and figure out what could have happened to it—before my pop finds out it's missing."

"You think someone took it?"

"I sure don't know what else to think," said Michael.

Lisa could still hear Jessica's voice suggesting to Michael that she, Lisa, had stolen the ring. She decided not to let Michael know she'd overheard the conversation. She was sure he didn't believe Jessica. He was just anxious to solve the mystery and she certainly wanted to help him all she could.

"If you think someone took it," said Lisa, "it must have been somebody who was on board."

"Well, there were The Fathers—we can cross them off the list—and you and me. We can cross us off the list, too—can't we, Lisa?"

Lisa flushed at his questioning tone. She felt guilty about the knowledge she had of Jessica's accusations.

"Of course," she said. "So the only others here were the two customs men."

"They didn't even leave the cockpit. Remember, *you're* the one who said how odd it was they didn't search below."

"Yeah, that's right. Like I said, Michael, we have to think maybe, just maybe, you took the ring off the hook and left it somewhere else. How about when you were helping your pop with the ship's papers? Could it somehow have gotten mixed up with them?"

"Hardly. Pop and I decided to neaten up all the stuff and, after we had everything sorted out, we put it in a waterproof Ziploc bag. It's transparent, so I'd have seen the ring if it was there."

"Would it hurt to look and check the plastic bag—or anywhere else you and the Skipper were working?"

"I guess not. I'll give a look. Why don't you search the galley once more? I hate the idea that someone stole it."

"Michael," said Lisa after they both finished fruitless searches, "someone else *was* aboard the boat."

"Oh? Who?"

"Jessica."

"You're not a bit of help! Jessica was standing alongside while the customs people were here—she wasn't aboard," he said with a sideways glance at Lisa.

"No, not then. But she was in the galley when I got here—when you came back to change your clothes and were looking for your racket—or said you were."

"Lisa, don't try to blame Jessica. The minute we got to *Dream Weaver* I ran ahead and looked on the hook. I saw that the ring wasn't there long before Jessica even came below."

"Well, who or what can we blame? I just don't know what to think anymore."

"Lisa," said Michael, "you've got to help me find my ring! This is terrible, but . . . but are you sure that you don't know anything about it?"

"What do you mean?"

"I mean . . . well . . . well, maybe you know where it is and you're embarrassed to tell me. Aw, heck, Lisa—I don't know how to say it. I was just thinking that you were—"

"What you're trying to say is that you think I took your ring?"

"I don't know what to think, it's just that—"

"It's just that Jessica told you I took it!"

Michael looked at Lisa in amazement. "You heard us talking? Is that why you hit her?"

"I told you! I didn't hit her on purpose."

"Okay, okay. But you did hear what she said?"

"Yes, I heard her accusing me. But I sure didn't think you believed her."

"I didn't believe her then. But now, Lisa, I don't know what to believe. *You* knew exactly where I put the ring."

"I didn't do it, Michael! You have no right to think I did. What would I want with your ring?"

"How should I know, Lisa? You told me you were always broke. Maybe when I told you pop said I might hock it—well, maybe that gave you an idea of how to get some extra dough." He looked at the purse she had clutched in her hand—and gazed at her with questioning eyes.

"Stop it, Michael," Lisa shrieked. "Just stop it this minute! I don't know where your stupid ring is, and I don't care."

"Come on, Lisa, let's talk about this without you having hysterics."

"I don't want to talk to you, and I don't want you to talk to me ever again!

"That'll be hard to do—on a boat together for a month."

"We'll see about that! Just you leave me alone. I hate you, Michael Montgomery!"

Lisa picked up her purse and stormed off

the boat. Heartbreaking sobs racked her body. She liked Michael so much, how could he possibly think she'd stolen his ring? The harder she cried, the faster she ran down the concrete pier. Blinded by tears, she bumped smack into someone. It was the tall customs man who had been so kind to her when he was on *Dream Weaver*.

"Take care there, Little Miss," he said in his British accent. "You almost knocked me into the water."

"I'm so sorry, Sir. I wasn't watching where I was going."

"No harm done. You look hot and bothered. Been playing tennis?" he asked as he noticed the outfit she still wore.

As they talked, a great scheme popped into Lisa's mind.

"Gosh, I'm glad I bumped into you," she said. "I need to know something. Maybe you can help me."

"I'll surely try."

"If someone wanted to go home from here, how would they do it?"

"You want to go home? And not on the boat that brought you?"

"I was just wondering—suppose my mom got sick or something and I had to get home in a hurry. What would I do?"

"Well, you could fly to Miami. There are several airports in the Abacos—most of the flights for the States leave from Marsh Harbour."

"I mean, how could I get away from here, from West End. All the tourists didn't come by boat, did they?"

"Oh, no, most of them are Canadians. We have several flights to Canada every day."

"Canada! That's great! Do you know how much it costs, when the planes leave?"

"Slow down, Little Miss. You're not planning to run away from your folks, are you?"

"Oh, no," lied Lisa. "Like I told you, I was just wondering."

"Well, in that case, you can get all the information you need at the front desk in the hotel. And don't forget—you'll need to turn in your immigration card at the airport—in case you leave."

"Thanks a lot, Sir. And next time I see you, I'll try not to run you down."

Lisa could almost hear her mother cautioning her not to go into that plush hotel wearing a tennis dress and sneakers, so she headed for the boat to change clothes—and figure out how to avoid even looking at Michael.

When she boarded *Dream Weaver*, she found The Fathers in the salon playing backgammon. Michael was glumly slumped in a chair, absentmindedly thumbing through a magazine. He looked at her beseechingly.

"Lisa, I've got to talk to you," he pleaded.

Her resolve almost weakened at his woebegone look. But she managed to ignore him and rushed past him to her cabin.

She flopped down on the bunk, buried her face in a pillow and cried. She wept with yearning for Michael's friendship and trust. She wept with hurt at his suspicions. She wept with anger at Jessica's accusations and her obvious flirtation with Michael. Lisa sobbed so hard and so long that she fell into an exhausted sleep.

When she awoke it was already dark. Her dad was calling to her that he hoped she was getting dressed. He said they were all going to the hotel for dinner in about a half hour.

"Okay if I skip it?" asked Lisa, as she stood in her cabin doorway.

"Of course it's not okay. We're all eating together tonight. Hurry and change your clothes. And, Lisa, do something with your hair and face. What's the matter with you? Have you been crying?"

"I took a nap and just woke up. Honest, Dad, I'm not hungry and I don't feel like being with people."

"Okay, okay, Lisa, suit yourself. But for heaven's sake, pull yourself together—you look awful."

When she was sure that The Fathers and Michael were safely out of the way and probably seated in the dining room, Lisa walked to the large hotel. The lobby was crowded with excited people and stacks of luggage. Lines of men and women were spiraling out from the long reception desk. Lisa felt foolish standing there in the middle of all the confusion, so she got on the end of a line of waiting people.

A grandmotherly woman standing next to Lisa smiled at her and asked, "Were you supposed to fly out tonight, too?"

"Well, no, I just want to try and get a reservation to Canada for tomorrow."

"Oh, honey," said the woman, "I don't think that will be possible—all these folks are doing the same thing. No Canadian planes left today, you know."

"Why not?" asked Lisa.

"There was a strike of some sort. It's settled now, but there won't be any planes until tomorrow."

"Oh, heck, I was hoping I could go home tomorrow."

"That's too bad. Where's home?"

"Exeter, New Hampshire. But my mom

could meet me in Quebec, we visit there all the time."

"Look, there's another line starting," the woman said. "Let's hurry over there and get in it."

Just as they approached the next group of standees, Lisa saw her dad coming out of a phone booth.

There was no escaping him!

"Lisa, what on earth are you doing here? I thought you didn't want to be with people!" His critical eye glanced at her disheveled tennis outfit and her tear-reddened eyes.

Oh, boy, thought Lisa, this is the pits, what a mess.

"I'm just looking around," she said, evasively.

"I hope you had something to eat. Our meal was terrible—the dining room was mobbed and the service was awful."

"I told you, I wasn't hungry. I just felt like—"

Lisa was mentally fishing for an adequate excuse when the elderly woman came over.

"There you are, young lady. I have to run along, but I wanted to tell you I got my reservation to Montreal for early tomorrow. I asked about Quebec for you—there are still some seats left on the late afternoon flight. You'd better get back in line if you want one."

"Gee, that's great. Umm—I'm still thinking about it. Thanks a lot, anyhow."

"Lisa, what's going on here? Why are you thinking about a plane reservation?" demanded her dad.

Lisa pushed up her glasses and looked at him earnestly.

"Dad, I want to go home." Her voice quavered.

"Go home? Lisa, what's the matter with you? Let's sit down and talk about this."

He led the already weeping Lisa across the lobby to a comfortable couch. He turned toward her, wiped her eyes with his hanky and took her hand. "Now tell me all about it, Pet. What's your problem?" he asked gently.

"There's no problem, Dad. I just want to go home."

"But you've only been away a few days! Are you homesick?"

"Nope. But I'm not having a good time and I want to leave. I could call mom and have her meet me in Quebec—if you'd give me the money for a ticket."

"But why, Lisa? Are you upset with me? Am I bugging you with my cracks about your mother? I know I shouldn't do that, but I don't like the way she's encouraging you to take yourself so seriously."

"I hate to hear you put her down. But she

says mean things about you, too, and I don't like that either. There's nothing I can do about it, I guess." She sighed at the enormity of this grown-up problem—and at the devastating problem of her broken friendship with Michael.

"What is it then, Pet?" he asked softly. "Should I get off your back about your clothes and being more like other kids?"

"Oh, Dad, it has nothing to do with *you*. Please don't make a big deal out of it. Just let me go home!"

"But, Lisa, I have to know why."

"I can't tell you why. Just—just because, that's all."

"I simply don't understand you! Our cruise has hardly begun. We haven't seen or done any of the great things we planned. And what about Michael? I thought you liked him and you were having fun together."

"Michael's swell. Only now he—"

"Is it that Jessica person? Is she upsetting you, are you jealous of her?"

"Oh, Dad," Lisa wept, "I just can't talk about it. Please, please, let me go home. All you have to do is give me the money and get my immigration card back from the Skipper."

"And what am I supposed to tell him—and Michael?"

"Tell them anything—tell them I'm homesick. Only just help me get away from here—quick."

"Okay, I give up, Lisa. You seem to have it all figured out. I'll make a deal with you. We're going to be stuck here tomorrow. There's a front moving in with high winds and rain, and the Skipper doesn't want to sail into the storms. So you sleep on it tonight. I'd still like to know what you're running away from. Maybe you can tell me about it tomorrow when you've calmed down. We'll have all day to do something about your going home—unless you change your mind, of course."

"I won't change my mind. I swear I won't."

"We'll see. Let's go back to *Dream Weaver* now and see what the others are up to. Please, try not to look so gloomy, Lisa."

"I'll stay out of everyone's sight, you'd better believe it! I'll just go to my cabin and read."

Lisa decided she ought to write a farewell note to Michael. She sat at the small desk-dressing table in her cabin and tried to put her thoughts on paper. She couldn't compose a letter because she couldn't compose her mind —which had slipped into a daydream about Michael.

She pictured him opening the letter. He would be very upset. He would remember their hours of companionship, their friendly talks, their intimate exchanges of confidences. He would recall how he admired her long hair blowing in the wind, and how great she looked in her tennis clothes.

In her fantasy Lisa could still hear Michael saying, "She's a great kid." Yes, she reflected, after she left tomorrow, Michael would realize that she couldn't possibly have stolen his ring. And he would be very sorry she was gone.

Lisa's stationery was covered with the doodles she unconsciously drew: hearts with the initials "M.M." and "L.H." and "Michael Montgomery" written dozens of times—even "Lisa Montgomery" and "Lisa Harwood Montgomery." The inked scribbles were smudged by her free-flowing tears.

Maybe, her reverie continued, maybe, he'll find the ring tonight. Or tomorrow, right before she got on the plane. He would call out to her to come back. She would hear him from the plane's doorway and would run into his outstretched arms. She would let him nuzzle his face in her long hair. He would beg her to forgive him. And she would.

Suddenly, Lisa realized that all the water on her desk was not tears—rain was blowing through the hatch above her. As she reached up to close the opening, she saw jagged lightning flashes and heard enormous rolls of thunder. Even in her cozy cabin, she could hear the wind whipping the riggings of the boats in the marina. She could feel *Dream Weaver* rocking in the churning water.

Lisa was afraid—not only of the vicious storm outside, but also of the turmoil inside her mind and body.

Someone knocked on her cabin door.

"Lisa? Lisa, are you awake?" a voice whispered.

It was Michael! He had found his ring, she imagined, and he'd come to tell her how sorry he was, and how much he liked her and wanted to be friends again.

"Are you scared?" he asked.

"Of course not."

"Lisa, I've got to talk to you!"

"What about?"

"What we were talking about this afternoon. Tomorrow I'm gonna have to tell pop about my ring and I don't know what to say to him."

Lisa's heart sank. He hadn't found his ring. He still suspected her.

"I told you I never wanted to talk to you again! Leave me alone, Michael! Beat it! Beat it quick before I scream and The Fathers will come and I'll tell them you're trying to get in here to do something awful to me."

"Oh, Lisa, stop being so silly."

"I mean it, Michael." Her voice rose hysterically.

She sensed that he had left.

A few minutes later there was another knock.

"Go away, Michael," she shouted.

"Lisa, it's dad. I just came to see if you were okay. May I come in?"

"I guess so."

"Why did you think it was Michael?" he asked as he entered her cabin.

"I don't know. I just thought maybe it was."

"You're angry with him, aren't you? He's what you're running away from, isn't he?"

"I'm not running away. I just want to go home."

"Oh, Lisa, it's too late at night to argue. And you look all in. Do you think you can get some sleep?"

"I'm exhausted, but I'm not sleepy."

"Maybe some warm milk would help. By the way, did you eat any dinner tonight?"

Lisa realized she hadn't eaten a thing since she and Michael had sat on the seawall. That happy time seemed ages ago, instead of just this morning.

"I guess I could use some milk, or something."

"C'mon, I'll help you fix a bite."

"Is anyone out there?"

"You mean Michael? No."

The Skipper was sitting in the salon. Lisa smiled at him wanly as she moved around the galley.

"Fixing a peanut butter sandwich, Lisa?" he called to her.

"Oh, no," she said, unhappily.

"What do you feel like eating?" her dad asked.

"I'll just have some soup."

"Need any help?"

"Nope. Really, I'm okay, Dad. Thanks for reminding me that I was hungry."

She poured the soup into a bowl for heating in the microwave. But she lost her appetite when she saw the empty hook where Michael's ring had hung.

"Quite a storm out there, Lisa," said the Skipper.

"Sure is." She munched a few saltines and drank a glass of milk. She couldn't even swallow the soup. She threw it in the garbage bag. Her heart lurched with sadness as she remembered Michael describing how they'd get rid of the trash.

"By the way, Lisa," said the Skipper, "this storm will probably knock out all the power around here. Without our electric hook-up to the dock, we have to rely on the ship's batteries and generator. The only thing that'll be a problem is the hot water heater. There'll be enough to go around if we all take short showers. Okay?"

"Okay. Guess I'll go to bed now. 'Night, Dad. 'Night, Skipper."

Lisa awoke early and lay in her bunk listening to the wind and rain. She hoped the bad weather wouldn't stop the planes from flying. She was still determined to go home. She packed most of her gear in her duffle bag and laid out her traveling outfit.

Then she took a long, hot shower and washed her hair.

She heard the three males bustling around the galley so she stayed in her cabin until the breakfast noises stopped. As she ate more saltines and milk, she heard the Skipper yelling from his cabin in the aft end of the boat.

"Who used all the hot water?" he roared. "There isn't even enough for a shave."

No one answered him. He rushed into the galley and glared at Lisa.

"I guess I did, Skipper. I'm sorry. I forgot what you said about short showers."

"Listen, young lady, you and I are going to have a long talk," he stated firmly.

"Please don't yell at me, Skipper. I told you I was sorry."

"There's more to talk about than hot water! Come along with me."

Lisa followed him obediently. She perched meekly on the edge of the bunk in her cabin. The Skipper dropped his ample body into the chair at the desk. His glance swept over the piece of paper covered with Lisa's doodles.

"Okay, now tell me what this is all about," he said as he noticed the partially packed luggage.

"Didn't dad tell you? I'm going home today."

"He told me you *wanted* to go home. But he didn't tell me why—that's what I expect you to do."

"I can't, Skipper, I just can't."

"Please, Lisa, try to tell me about it. After all, I'm the captain of this vessel and I've got the right to know why a member of my crew is jumping ship." His grin was teasing, but his voice was stern.

"Jumping ship? Isn't that like mutiny? I know I disobeyed you about the hot water, but I've done everything else you've asked." She smiled at him weakly.

"It's the captain's job to see that everyone is content and in harmony. You're unhappy, you're not eating, you've apparently had a disagreement with Michael. Your gloomy behavior is affecting all the rest of us. And I want to know what's bugging you! What's with you and Michael?" he asked with solicitude.

"You'll have to ask him about that."

"But I'm asking *you;* I'll get to him later. Right now, he's gone out—"

"In this rain? Probably went to see if Jessica was scared of the storm," she said, bitterly.

"Actually, I sent him to the dockmaster's office to get the latest news on the weather. You just mentioned Jessica. Are you and Michael feuding over that miserable little girl?"

"She's not a little girl. She's, she's—oh, Skipper," Lisa burst into tears, "please leave me alone. I can't talk about it. Just let me go home—then you won't be bothered with my problems."

"Oh, Lisa, Lisa, you poor child." He sat beside her and held her in his arms. "Your problems don't bother me. I want to help you. Please talk to me—nothing can be as bad as you think."

"It's awful, Skipper, just awful," she sobbed into his chest. He had the same clean, soapy smell as his son—and this reminder of Michael made her weep even more bitterly.

"Tell me, Lisa, tell me, let me help you."

She pushed up her glasses and looked at him imploringly.

"I just can't tell you, Skipper. Michael would kill me if I told you about his ring. Oh, no, what have I said! Please don't make me talk about it."

He engulfed her in his arms. His voice was comforting and consoling, softly urging her to confide in him. Lisa couldn't resist his entreaties. Haltingly she tried to relate the whole story. He continued to comfort her as she struggled with her words and her emotions.

"Let's see if I've got this straight," he said gently. "Michael lost his ring—Jessica told him you could have stolen it—Michael didn't believe her—but then he couldn't find it—so he accused you of taking it—you had a fight—and that's why you want to go home. Is that right, Lisa?" Now the Skipper's tone was tight and angry.

"Sort of. But don't be mad at Michael. He feels awful already and he's scared to tell you about it. Honest, if I can just go home everything will be okay. Or maybe the ring will turn up someplace and Michael won't hate me anymore."

"I can't let Michael get away with such

behavior. He's made you miserable and I'm going to do something about it right now."

"Oh, Skipper, Michael will never forgive me for snitching on him—and I couldn't stand that. I like him so much and I want him to like me."

"Everything's okay now, Lisa. I understand the whole mess and I'll straighten it out. I'm going to talk to your dad now and—"

"Oh, m'gosh, he'll be so shook up when he knows I told you and not him."

"I don't think so. He'll understand that sometimes it's easier to confide in someone you don't know very well instead of someone you love very much."

"I sure hope so."

"Anyhow, why don't you get out of that housecoat and put on something bright and pretty. You've been sad long enough! When Michael comes back, we'll all get together and hash this out."

"I can't face Michael, Skipper—he'll know I told you everything."

"All we're going to do is straighten out this mystery. I promise you, when I yell at Michael, you won't hear it. Trust me, Lisa, everything will be okay now."

"If you say so. Only I don't see how."

"You will. You will. Just get yourself fixed

up and come to the salon. And, Lisa, please—not another shower!"

Lisa laughed for the first time in what seemed like years. Nothing had actually changed. But without even knowing why, she suddenly felt light-hearted and happy.

4

Dream *Weaver*'s salon seemed to Lisa like a dentist's waiting room.

Michael, slouched in a chair, looked straight ahead. His face was contorted in a painful expression—as though he were expecting to have ten fillings, without Novocain.

Lisa and her dad sat side by side on a small couch. He held her hand tightly as if to give her courage for the ordeal ahead. The Skipper came jauntily into the salon, like the dentist about to ask, "Who's next." He gave Lisa a big wink and seated himself in the plush captain's chair.

The wink told her that he approved of her changed appearance. She wore her new hot-pink jeans outfit. But Michael's downcast look depressed her, and she realized that she looked brighter then she felt. How much had the Skipper told Michael, she wondered.

"Michael, sit up straight," the Skipper commanded. "And get this straight, too," he continued. "I'm very upset with you. I know all about your ring. And I also know how badly you've treated Lisa."

"Aw, Pop," Michael protested. "Do we have to do this in front of the whole world?" Injury and resentment were reflected in his glance at Lisa.

"No, we'll have it out alone later, believe me. But there's one thing Lisa and her dad have to hear right now. And that's what happened to your ring."

"Pop, I don't know what happened to my ring. I'm afraid someone took it."

"Someone took it, all right. You know how I disapproved of your getting such an expensive class ring—"

"Yeah, yeah."

"You've been careless with it ever since you got it; left it lying around for anyone to pick up. So yesterday morning, when I saw it hanging there on the hook, I decided to teach you a lesson. I took your ring!

"You took it?" Lisa and Michael exclaimed in unison.

"Yes, and it's going to be a long while before you get it back. But your carelessness isn't the only trouble you've got, young man—"

"Please, Pop, not now. I've just got to talk to Lisa," he said in a remorseful voice.

"Yes, now! You can talk to Lisa later— if she'll talk to you after the way you hurt her."

Lisa knew she would. All she wanted to do was make up and be friends again.

"Come on, Lisa," said her dad, "walk to the hotel with me. I've got to make some phone calls."

"The rain's let up, but it still looks stormy," he said as they strolled along a path bordered with towering Australian pine trees. "Have you ever seen trees like this before?" he asked. "Their real name is Casuarina."

Lisa looked up at the graceful, feathery branches. Her dad seemed preoccupied, as if he had something on his mind. She wondered why he was making small talk. She bent over and picked up some of the tiny, symmetrical pine cones. As she stood up and pushed her glasses back up on her nose, she looked at him imploringly.

"Dad, are you mad at me 'cause I talked to the Skipper and not you."

"Oh, Pet, this has been a terrible experience for you. Why don't you try to put it out of your mind. Please don't brood over it or take it too seriously."

"Why won't you ever talk to me about anything serious? It's really important for me to know if you're angry about it."

"Lisa, I'm not mad at you. I'm upset—with myself, I mean. It's hard being a part-time father. This was my one chance to help you through something big, and I blew it."

"Oh, gosh, you didn't, Dad, you didn't. It's just that it's hard for me to talk to you. We're not together much, and when we are we're so busy having fun we don't get to know each other."

"I'm not sure I understand. You mean, since you've grown up—well, almost grown up— we've never shared any bad times? That's why you couldn't tell me about this?"

"That's it. I don't . . . I don't relate to you, even though you're my father."

"Oh, Lisa, you're such a funny, sweet, serious person," he said as he hugged her lovingly. "Where on earth did you learn that? Do you 'relate' to your mother?"

"I read lots of stuff, 'specially about getting along with people. And, Dad," she confided, "don't ever let mom know this 'cause she'd really be shook up. But I'd never have been able to talk to her—about Michael's ring and all."

"That's interesting. Why wouldn't you talk over your problems with her?"

"Oh, she'd make a big deal of it—like a church sermon, ya know? And . . . and she'd laugh at me for liking a boy I just met. But, honest, Dad I do like Michael a lot. He's the first kid I ever knew who I could talk to about *anything*. I guess it's because his parents are divorced, too. Except he doesn't even know his mother. Oh, I dunno, I can't think of how to say what I mean."

"Do you mean that now we're going to have a better relationship, we'll be able to communicate with each other?"

"Yeah, that's right, that's what I mean."

"You've been pretty confused since the divorce, haven't you, Lisa?"

"Yeah," she sighed. "Sometimes I think it's my fault."

"No, Pet, you were the reason we didn't split up sooner. And maybe that wasn't right, either."

"Yeah, I've read a lot of articles about that, too. I guess I'll get it all together some time."

"That's enough heavy talk for one day, Lisa. But let's be sure that this month together really changes our relationship. You'll see what a great father-mother I can be."

She sighed again. Right now the only relationship she wanted to change was her strained one with Michael.

"I'll just make one phone call, and then let's have lunch," her dad said.

She was looking in a gift shop window when he returned.

"Look at that, Lisa. That pin over there. It's a little gold pine cone—like the ones you just picked up. I'm going to get it for you, and when you wear it you'll be reminded of this conversation. Okay?"

"Great. I'd love to have it."

"And, listen, about lunch, I've got to hang around here and wait for my call to go through. Can you get along okay?"

Lisa was starved, but she was so anxious about her confrontation with Michael that she knew she'd never be able to eat, anyway.

"Oh, sure," she said. "I think I'll shop for a dress-up dress."

"Fine. Buy as much as you want. Just don't forget there's a limit to that credit card I gave you."

"I guess it'll get me through one day," Lisa teased him back.

"There, see—you're changing already. Yesterday you'd have said something like, 'Oh, I won't spend very much. I'm very practical.'"

"Well, I almost did say that. But I feel kinda

square in the clothes I brought along, and I'd love to get some new ones. Thanks, Dad. See ya later."

Lisa walked along the street of shops until she found her dream dress. It fell in soft, flouncy gauze folds. A kaleidoscope of pastel colors—like a melted rainbow.

In the dressing room she adjusted the full skirt and pulled the puckered top into place. She was pleased that the peasant-style bodice made her look more bosomy than she actually was. As she twirled and swirled in front of the three-way mirror she pictured herself dancing with Michael—maybe in the hotel—tonight. After they made up, of course.

While the saleslady made out a charge slip, Lisa looked out the boutique window. Through the glass she saw Michael entering a shop across the narrow street. She signed for her purchase, grabbed the package and ran toward the store where Michael was.

She jumped over a wide puddle of rain water. She landed flat on her feet, with most of her weight on her left foot—the same ankle she'd injured a few years ago. It hurt as much now as it had then. But her need to see Michael was stronger than the pain shooting up her leg.

Lisa hobbled into the store and leaned

against a counter near where Michael stood. She aimlessly studied a swimsuit display. As she held up a tiny string bikini, Michael came up to her.

"I don't like that one, Lisa." His voice was tentative and his look questioning.

"Oh? Jessica's is sorta like this—you seemed to go for it on her."

"Yeah, well, you're not Jessica's type." He picked up a red two-piece suit. "Here, this looks like you."

"I don't want to mess with a suit right now."

"Good. Lisa, let's go someplace and talk," he implored. "I've got a lot of things to say to you."

"Was it awful with your pop?" she asked as they left the store.

"Pretty bad. But I deserved . . . Lisa, why're you limping? What's the matter with your leg?"

"I hurt my ankle. Oh, Michael, it's killing me. I've got to sit down."

"You've got to see a doctor, at once. There's one down the block. Let's hope he's there today."

Michael practically carried her to the medical clinic. A nurse told them the doctor would be back soon. She gave Lisa a pill to relieve the pain.

They sat on a black leather couch in the waiting room, and Michael held Lisa's hand.

"Michael, you must be furious with me for squealing on you. I didn't mean to, but—"

"Yeah, I know. I was pretty teed off at first, but then I realized you probably couldn't help yourself once pop got you cornered."

"That's for sure!"

"Ya know, that guy could sell a freezer to an Eskimo. That's why he's such a great lawyer. Believe me, Lisa, I understand what must have happened and I sure don't blame you for telling him."

"That's a relief! I felt awful about it."

"I was gonna tell him the whole story anyhow—as soon as I got the guts to do it. Geez, Lisa, I almost died when pop told me you wanted to go home. I'd have confessed a lot sooner if I'd known you were even thinking about such a thing."

Michael reached out and pushed up Lisa's glasses and put some strands of her hair back in place. His hand lingered on her shiny head, then it cradled her face gently and held up her chin so that their eyes met. "Lisa, can you ever forgive me?"

"It was so gross, Michael. How could you have thought it was me?"

"I just don't know. All I know is I'm sorrier

than I could ever tell you. You're such a great kid, I don't know how I could ever have hurt you that way. Please, Lisa, say you forgive me and then let's try and forget about it."

Michael's voice was unsteady and his eyes filled with tears. The only other time Lisa had seen a man cry was after the divorce when her dad kissed her good-bye. Her heart felt as squishy now as it had then.

"Of course I forgive you. Anyhow, if it hadn't been for that awful Jessica, you'd never have done it. Like you said—let's forget it."

Lisa wasn't sure that the doctor's advice was worth twenty-five dollars of her dad's money: "Stay off your feet, use a cane, wrap in elastic bandage, the nurse'll give you some pills for pain." She knew she should have paid more attention to what he said. But all she could think of was that now she and Michael couldn't go dancing—and he wouldn't see her fantastic new dress.

"Hey, Lisa, I saw a neat cane in the hotel souvenir shop. I'm going to run over there and get it for you," Michael said. "I'll be back in a flash."

"It really is neat," Lisa exclaimed, when he came back with the heavy, transparent Lucite cane filled with pastel-colored artificial flowers. "I love it!"

Michael went to another counter and selected a dainty deep-pink silk hibiscus on a comb. He shyly gave Lisa the flower and told her how pretty it would look in her hair. "I'll find you a fresh one every day we're in the islands," he promised.

"Michael, I'm absolutely starving to death," declared Lisa when she spied the coffee shop.

They devoured foot-long hot dogs and creamy milk shakes. "I feel better now," she said. "I really feel great!"

"You know, Lisa, pop really let me have it about the ring. But he was even madder about you. He thinks you're super special—and so do I."

"I'm glad you feel that way, Michael. I like you, lots, too." They looked at each other tenderly for a moment and Lisa knew that the incident of the ring was truly behind them.

Suddenly loud laughter filled the room.

Jessica!

Lisa would have recognized that husky sound anywhere. Jessica even laughed with a southern accent.

"Hey, there, Michael, how ya doin'?" She looked at his left hand. "You didn't find your ring, I see."

There was a long pause. Lisa watched Michael's handsome face blush right through its suntan.

"Yeah," he muttered, "I found it. I'm gonna leave it on the boat so I won't lose it again. We're just leaving, Jessica—see ya around." He helped Lisa out of her chair and handed her the colorful cane. "Lisa sprained her ankle. We've got to go now. C'mon, Lisa."

"I guess Lisa can't go dancing tonight," Jessica called after them.

"Not a chance, but we'll probably eat in the hotel anyhow."

Back at *Dream Weaver*, The Fathers were aghast at Lisa's injury. She was quick to tell them how Michael had rushed her to the doctor. They smothered her with attention, and insisted that she go to bed.

As she drifted off to sleep, she heard Michael saying, "But she's got a new dress. It'll be okay just to go eat in the hotel. If she's hurting, we'll leave. And the doc gave her some pain pills if she needs 'em."

"But she can't walk all the way over there," the Skipper protested.

"Well, if they've got their hearts set on it, let 'em go," Lisa heard her dad say. "I've got an idea—we'll rent them a golf cart for the evening."

When Lisa reappeared in the salon she was greeted by whistles of approval from the three men.

She knew that the colorful dress flattered her figure. She had put up her gleaming hair in a twist with Michael's flower tucked in the middle. Her large brown eyes behind her stylish glasses sparkled with anticipation. No one even noticed that she wore pink Angel Tread bedroom slippers because of her swollen foot.

"You take good care of her, Michael," admonished Lisa's dad.

"And get back early," said the Skipper. "We're leaving at the crack of dawn no matter what the weather's like."

The Fathers set off for a taxi to take them to the casino in nearby Freeport. Lisa and Michael rode to the hotel in an electric golf cart.

As they entered the lobby, Lisa saw Jessica and her friends climbing the wide, circular staircase to the dining room.

"I don't think I can manage all those steps, Michael."

"You don't have to. We'll take the elevator." He pointed to the large glass cage that glittered with multicolored lights.

Seated at an intimate candlelit table, they studied the huge French menu.

"I'll have the *potage aux pommes de terre*," Lisa said. "And I'll try *soupe a l'oignon*," Michael told the waiter. As they enjoyed their soups—Lisa's potato and Michael's onion—they were served a *salade de champignons* in a gleaming glass dish. Michael piled the marinated mushrooms onto each salad plate.

When Michael's *coq au vin* was placed before him, he dug into the tender chicken with enthusiasm. Lisa appreciated the *gigot roti a l'ail.* But she picked at her lamb because she was so aware of Jessica's presence in the dining room. Just as they finished their desserts of *eclairs* and *meringues,* the native band started up.

Michael pulled his chair close to Lisa's. He put his arm around her shoulder. She felt warm and cherished. They listened to the sensuous music and chatted idly about the ornate room and the well-dressed people in it.

Lisa knew that the spell would be broken when Jessica slithered toward their table. She wore a clingy white sheath with slits up to her thighs.

"How about a dance, Michael?"

"Not now, Jessica."

"Aw, just one, Michael. This music's too good to miss," she wheedled. "You won't mind, will you, Lisa? Oh, how's your ankle?" she asked with false solicitude.

"Fine."

"Jessica, I don't want to leave Lisa alone. We'll dance some other time."

"David's with me—I'll get him to babysit with Lisa."

"Would you mind, Lisa?" asked Michael.

"I guess not," said Lisa somewhat ungraciously.

Jessica shoved David into the chair next to Lisa. She tugged Michael off to the dance floor. "Has anyone ever told you how handsome you are? You—"

Lisa was glad the music drowned out the rest of Jessica's conversation.

"That Jessica's a character, isn't she?" said David.

"Yeah. Listen, you don't have to sit here. I'm okay."

"Gosh, I don't mind. Man, you look fantastic!"

"Thanks. Did you see my cane?"

"It's somethin' else. Talk to me some more—your accent sends me. I'm going to Yale, so I'd better get used to you Yankees."

"Yale? That's super. I'm at Dexter—lots of our boys go to Yale."

"Hey, that's a great prep school. I didn't know it was coed."

"Has been for ages. But, boy, is it rough. I don't know if I'll ever get out of there! I want to go to Harvard or MIT."

"Wow!"

"They're the best for computer engineering. That's—what's so funny about that? Why're you laughing?"

"Not at you, Lisa. Just a few minutes ago Jessica told me she was going to—heck, I can't think of the name of it—anyhow, it's supposed to be the playground of Florida. You know the college I mean, don't you, Lisa?"

"I never heard of it." Lisa's quick mind wondered how far it was from Tallahassee, where Michael would be.

"I asked Jessica what she was going to major in," David continued. "She told me 'boys'—I'd say she's off to a good start."

Lisa followed his gaze to the couple on the dance floor. Their bodies flowed rhythmically to the pulsating disco beat. She unconsciously tapped her feet to the music. Pain stabbed her leg and she realized that her medication had worn off.

Even after she took another pill she still felt awful. She was dizzy and nauseated, and wondered if she could make it to the ladies room.

"Are you okay?" said David.

"Would you get Michael? I've got to get back to the boat, in a hurry." She took several deep breaths and the queasiness left her stomach. But she felt as though she were on fire, and she itched all over.

"What's the matter, Lisa?" asked Michael. "Are you sick? Gee, you look kind of green."

"Probably green with envy because she watched us dance," taunted Jessica.

"Oh, bug off, Jessica," snapped Michael. "Can't you see that Lisa's really sick?"

5

Two days and lots of sleep later, Lisa realized that whatever had been wrong with her wasn't wrong with her anymore.

She stepped from her bunk and cautiously put some weight on the bandaged ankle. It felt almost normal. Her spirits lifted.

As she finished tucking a T-shirt into her shorts, she heard Michael telling someone he was going to fix some soup and toast for Lisa.

"Ugh, soup," she said as she left her cabin and entered the galley. "I'm awfully fuzzy about what's been going on, but I *do* know that you and The Fathers have fed me enough soup to last the rest of my life."

"Lisa, what're you doing up?" Michael said. He put his arm around her. "Man, it's good to see you looking healthy again. How do you feel?"

"I feel like Rip Van Winkle—and also like a cheeseburger, some fries and a chocolate shake."

"Gee, I'd better check that out with The Fathers."

"Tell them you've got to feed me or I'll die of starvation."

"Oh, Pet, I was so worried about you," said her dad as he came into the galley and held her in his arms. "Are you sure you should be up?"

"I feel super—except I'm awfully hungry."

"Your stuff'll be ready in a few minutes," said Michael. He moved from freezer to microwave and Lisa knew her order was being filled efficiently.

"Where's the Skipper? Where are we? What was the matter with me?"

"Pop's driving the boat."

"If you feel okay, Lisa," her dad said, "let's go topside and we'll tell you all about it. You can listen while you eat."

He helped her up the ladder to the cockpit and Michael followed with the tray of food.

"Well, if it isn't Sleeping Beauty," said the

Skipper. He let go of the large chrome steering wheel long enough to embrace her and arrange a comfortable seat of boat cushions for her.

"Wow," said Michael as he watched her dig into the plentiful plate of food, "you really are awake now, aren't you? For the last couple of days you've been so sleepy and groggy, The Fathers and I thought we were taking care of a doll."

"You sure must have been good nurses," she said, "because I'm all better now—but I'd sure like to know what happened."

Michael told her that by the time they had left the hotel and had returned to *Dream Weaver*, she had a fever and had broken out in a rash. He said that The Fathers had decided she was in shock from the pain of her ankle injury and just needed a good night's sleep.

"So," the Skipper picked up the story, "we let you sleep while we got underway. There hasn't been enough wind to fill the sails since we left West End, and we've been under power all the way—except when we anchored last night."

"Yeah," said Lisa, "the sound of the engine kept putting me to sleep. Just the way I always fall asleep on a plane once it takes off."

"The drone of the engine wasn't all that put

you to sleep," said her dad. "By morning, yesterday, your fever was up, your face was swollen and you complained about itching all over—"

"So pop got out his *First Aid Afloat* book," interrupted Michael, "and he looked up all your symptoms. He suspected maybe you had food poisoning—"

"Oh, no, that meal was super," said Lisa.

"Yeah, well, the symptoms didn't fit food poisoning, anyhow. So then pop decided it was an allergy of some sort."

"But I haven't got any allergies."

"There could have been something in the food," her dad said. "Seasoning or whatever, that you're not used to."

"So," said the Skipper, "I dosed you with the antihistamine I keep in *Dream Weaver*'s first aid kit."

"And that's what made me sleepy?"

"Right," the Skipper said. "While we were at anchor last night you seemed better and we figured the stuff had done its work."

"Yeah," said Lisa, "I remember thinking I was better. And then dad sponged me with cool water, didn't he?"

"And that was when you complained about your ankle hurting," said Michael. "So they gave you one of the doctor's pain pills."

"And then the Skipper bandaged my foot. I remember that."

"During the night," Michael said, "you started all over again—fever, itching, swelling. It was so awful, Lisa. I felt so sorry for you."

"That's right," said her dad, "you were getting worse instead of better. And we were helpless there, out in the middle of nowhere."

"Your dad got a good idea," said the Skipper. "He took a look at the doctor's pill bottle. The label didn't give the name of the medication, just directions to take for pain as needed."

"That was when I decided your problem was a reaction to the pills," said her dad. "So I gave you huge doses of antihistamine. That's what made you sleep most of today."

"What time is it anyway?"

"Sixteen hundred."

"Wow, four in the afternoon already!" Lisa hoped Michael was impressed that she understood how the twenty-four hour clock worked.

"Boy," she continued. "I sure kept you three busy, didn't I? Thanks a lot for taking care of me." She smiled at each of them. "Where are we now."

"We're just about here, at Manjack Cay." Michael picked up the nautical chart and pointed to the outline of land on the map.

"The water sure is clear, and a beautiful color."

"Yeah, it's shallow and protected in here. But look over there to your left, Lisa, down that channel at the end of the Cay."

"I see what you mean. Man, that looks wild. Look at the huge waves."

"That's the Atlantic Ocean and the waves are breaking on the barrier coral reefs that run along the outside of the Cays."

"Is that where we're going?"

"We're heading to Green Turtle Cay, should be there in an hour or so. We'll anchor here," he showed her the spot on the chart, "in a sheltered harbor. But see how close the ocean is on the other side of Green Turtle? We'll go over there—if you can walk, that is."

"Of course I can walk. Anyhow, I've got my cane—and this neat bandage."

She stuck out her leg. She hoped no one else noticed how red it was.

"Lisa," said Michael, "look at you. Gosh, you're all red again and you're shivering. But not the way it was before."

Her dad poked her flesh here and there. "Young lady, you're sunburned!"

"Oh, no," she wailed. "I forgot all about my Paba stuff. This is awful—I'm going to peel all over."

"C'mon below, Lisa," said Michael. "I'll fix

you up." He opened a bottle of white vinegar and slathered it on every bit of her exposed skin.

"This is what we Florida lifeguards use," he said. "It tans you fast and keeps you from peeling. Close your eyes, this stuff stings."

"I never get tan, but I'll be glad if I don't peel." She pictured how awful she'd look all scaley in her new clothes. "Gosh, I smell like a tossed salad."

"Yeah, you're some tomato!" Michael said.

That sounded like something he'd say to Jessica and it made Lisa ask, "I wonder where *Happy Daze* is?"

"Probably beat us to Green Turtle—they make better speed than we do."

Her dad called down from the cockpit to check on her sunburn. She said she was okay but was getting sleepy again. He told her to try to stay awake till bedtime so she'd get back on a regular schedule.

"We'll be there pretty soon," Michael said, "then you'll wake up. Once you asked me about the history of the Abacos—how about a history lesson now?"

"Okay. I love history. That's why I'm going to type the prof's book this summer—it's about the American Revolution."

"Then you should be interested in this. Many of the people in these islands are descendents—Loyalists from the American colonies who wanted to remain under the British Crown, and fled here for refuge when we won our independence."

"So that's why so many people we've met have such fantastic English accents."

"Yeah, and during the Civil War, too, the southern farmers brought their slaves, their livestock, everything to re-establish their way of life in the Bahamian Islands."

"Say, you're really up on this history."

"I like to find out all about places I visit," Michael said. He went on to tell her that the whole works was under Great Britian's rule until 1973, when the Bahamas became independent.

"Who was here before the English?"

"Way back in the sixteenth century, the Arawak Indians lived here, then it was taken over by the Spanish. Wait'll you hear some of the words we use now that're left over from the Indian culture: avocado, barbecue, cay, guava, hurricane, maize, potato, tobacco."

"No kidding. Hey, Michael, the boat's slowed down, we must be at Green Turtle. Let's go topside and watch. We'll finish the history lesson later, okay? It's fascinating."

"Okay, but you be sure and sit on the shady side."

The Skipper was at the helm, carefully

steering *Dream Weaver* parallel to the steep cliffs that were blanketed in all shades of green. As he turned the boat around a point of land he said, "Michael, you'd better go up on the bow and be the lookout." The Skipper explained to Lisa that Michael's polarized sunglasses would help him read the water— see the sandy shallow spots on which the boat might go aground.

The Skipper threaded his boat through the narrow channel and Lisa watched tiny houses and docks and small boats that lined the shore. They entered a wide harbor where numerous boats swung on their anchors.

"Hey, there's *Happy Daze*," Michael pointed to the large houseboat tied up at the Green Turtle Marina.

"Good, let 'em stay there. We want to pick an uncrowded quiet spot," said the Skipper. "There's a nice one."

They anchored in the lee of Big Bluff, a tree-covered hill.

The Fathers disappeared into the engine room to investigate what they told Lisa was "an ominous clank" in the diesel engine.

Michael and Lisa neatened up the galley after a light meal of pizza and salad, then sat on deck in the afterglow of the sunset.

"Time for your last vinegar bath," Michael told her. He doused her arms and legs with the smelly stuff. He had just begun to dab it on her beet-red face when the calm of the evening was shattered by the roar of a motorboat weaving around the anchored boats toward *Dream Weaver*.

It was Jessica in *Happy Daze'* dinghy—if such a large Boston Whaler and powerful motor could be called a dinghy, thought Lisa.

"Hey, y'all, thought you'd never get here. How ya doin', Michael?"

"Okay."

"I see you caught yourself an scrawny lobster," said Jessica as she examined Lisa's sunburned body.

Was it vinegar or anger that brought tears to Lisa's eyes?

6

Gee, where does the time go? We've been busy the last few days, but if anyone asked me exactly what we did, I couldn't tell 'em," Lisa said to Michael.

"Yeah, that's what's so great about cruising —you get so relaxed you hardly know or care what day it is."

The Fathers had rigged up an awning over the cockpit and Michael and Lisa sat in its shade, each writing picture postcards.

Lisa looked dreamily toward the shore and up at the high bluff they had climbed yesterday. She thought back about that experience. At first she hadn't been sure she could make the climb, even with her cane and Michael's strong arm steadying her. But then they'd found a gently sloping path that led to the top of the cliff.

"It's eighty-three feet high," Michael told her when they had reached the top, "just about the highest spot in the Abacos."

"It's so beautiful—the water looks like a mirror, smooth as glass."

As she looked southward from the high cliff all she saw was the vast expanse of green water punctuated here and there with small cays and rocks. She and Michael glimpsed New Plymouth Settlement. The height and distance made the village seem like a miniature town built around a model train set.

Behind them, in the water below, they could see *Dream Weaver*. She and all the other boats reminded Lisa of toy boats in the bathtub. Way off in the distance was the sparkling sapphire-blue Atlantic with its waves crashing onto the coral reefs.

"Even *Happy Daze* looks small from up here." She knew that Michael must have caught the bitterness in her voice.

"Don't let Jessica bug you," he said. "She's harmless."

"You mean 'harmless' like a snake?"

"Aw, c'mon, Lisa, try to understand her. She's just a girl who needs attention all the time."

"Yeah, well, she sure got your attention."

"Oh, she's kinda fun to be around—for a little while, anyhow."

Lisa pushed her huge sunglasses further up her nose and looked at Michael very seriously. "Listen, I've done a lot of thinking these past few days. And I've decided that I've had it with Jessica! From now on I'm staying as far away from her as I can."

"If that's how you want to handle it, be my guest. But, you know, we'll probably run into *Happy Daze* every place we go."

"Well, she'd better just stay out of my way."

Michael had taken off his soft, white cotton shirt and wrapped it carefully around Lisa's shoulders and arms to protect them from the sun. Her heart had jumped a little as he'd tied the long sleeves around her neck. They had walked back down the hill and his hand had felt tight and warm in hers.

Now, they sat in companionate silence, each intent on writing their "wish-you-were-here" postcards. Lisa still wore Michael's shirt. She'd keep it forever, she decided, as she rolled up the sleeves.

"Hot, isn't it?" said Michael. "Feel like a swim?"

"Sounds great. Where?"

"Over on the ocean side. It's a long, hilly walk, but I was talking to a guy in the marina and he said I could borrow his jeep for a coupla hours. I'll call him on the CB and see if it's okay."

"Seems funny to use the citizens' band radio instead of the phone," commented Lisa.

They loaded *Dream Weaver*'s dinghy with snorkeling and scuba gear and rowed the short distance across the water from their boat to the marina. As they tied up, the jeep's owner asked if they'd mind taking along some other kids.

Before they could answer, Jessica and her three friends spilled out of *Happy Daze* and piled into the jeep.

Jessica chattered about her doings as Michael drove the overcrowded vehicle through the plush landscaped grounds of the Green Turtle Club. The narrow trail took them uphill through a dense growth of low trees and shrubs. Lisa was intrigued by the hundreds of small land crabs that scurried across the jeep's path. The thicket ended abruptly. Michael parked and everyone ran across the sand dunes, through growths of sea oats and palm trees of every variety.

Lisa gasped with delight as she caught sight of the long white sandy beach. Like tons of sugar, she thought. Right past where she stood, Lisa noticed that the jagged coral barrier reef ran very close to the sand.

"C'mon, Lisa," called Michael. "We're going to swim outside the reef. This is a great place for snorkeling, too. It's one of the few spots in the Bahamas where you can swim right out to the reefs."

Lisa put on a face mask, snorkle and flippers. But Jessica and her gang were clowning around and disturbing the water so that Lisa couldn't see a thing below the surface.

"Michael, let's take our tanks and get away from all this confusion. I'm dying to see what's around here."

"Okay, but let's be sure to stay close together."

Lisa was awed by the marine world she discovered in and around the spectacular coral formations. Rainbow-hued tropical fish swam through colorful undersea gardens. She saw a huge starfish lolling on the sandy bottom. A moray eel slithered from behind a rock, and Lisa got out of its path fast. She was intrigued by the round, blackish sea urchins, some golfball size, some as big as baseballs. They squatted in plants, on the sand, in the angles of coral branches, and their long sharp needles extended in all directions like porcupine quills.

The spell was broken when Michael tapped his air indicator and pointed to hers to remind her that their air was getting low, and it was time to leave this undersea paradise. As they left the water, they stopped near some rocks to remove their diving gear. Lisa noticed the antennae of several spiney lobsters wiggling above the rocks' edges.

The other kids ran across the sand to where Michael and Lisa were slipping out of their flippers. Lisa noticed that Jessica's body in its bikini was almost as bare as her feet.

Suddenly, Jessica screamed. She lifted a bare foot from behind one of the rocks. Attached to her red-polished big toe was the claw of an equally red spiney lobster.

"Hey, Jessica," Lisa said, "I see you've caught yourself a scrawny lobster."

Lisa knew she should be ashamed of herself for taunting Jessica. But she just had to get even with her somehow. As Lisa wrapped herself in Michael's shirt, she noticed him looking at her with an amused expression. Then he gave her a long, conspiratorial wink! That made her rudeness worth it, she thought to herself.

The jeep ride back to the marina was very subdued.

The Fathers told Michael and Lisa they wouldn't be aboard for dinner—they were going to eat with some friends at the Bluff

Club. As the men waited for the club launch to come to *Dream Weaver* to pick them up, Lisa's dad asked her if she'd phoned her mother yet.

"Nope, but I sent her a card."

"Well, you could be home before that gets there. Next time you go ashore you'd better give her a call. I'm sure she misses you," he said.

Lisa was amazed at his concern for her mom's feelings. Maybe he doesn't really hate her as much as she thought, she said to herself. Maybe he's still in love with her, she daydreamed, and they'll get married again. She looked down at the gold pine cone pin her dad had given her—she wore it all the time, even on Michael's beloved shirt. The pin reminded her of her new understanding of where her father was coming from. What a silly idea, she thought. Of course they couldn't get married again. They're still the same people they always were. She decided that it was her own attitude toward each of them that was changing.

"C'mon, Lisa, stop daydreaming. The fire's ready and it's time to put on the meat." Michael had clamped a charcoal grill on *Dream Weaver's* stern. They shared a steak, salad and a long loaf of garlic bread.

"Michael, I've gotta try and call my mom. Would you mind dinking me ashore?"

"Oh, sure. Hey, why don't you put on a dress and we'll go to the Green Turtle Club. Things don't get rolling there till a little later, maybe we can go watch the sunset someplace."

"What's at the Green Turtle Club?"

"It's kind of a hangout for the skippers and crews of boats in the harbor and local kids go there, too. I'll bring my guitar. They've got an island combo, but anyone who wants can join in."

They tied up the dinghy at a low dock made just for that purpose. "Do you think it's safe to leave your guitar in the dink?" Lisa asked.

"Of course. Haven't you noticed how friendly and helpful the people are?"

Lisa went into the club office and placed her call—reversing the charges, of course. But her mom wasn't home.

"Let's walk up to Coco Bay," suggested Michael. "It's close by, not nearly as far as to the beach."

They strolled through the softly lighted club grounds. The evening air was scented with fragrant oleanders; the tiny white flowers of carissa shrubs gave out a delicate perfume. The tall, spikey Spanish Bayonet plants were in bloom and their large milky clusters of flowers poured out a heady essence.

Michael plucked a red hibiscus from one of the many shrubs along the path. He shyly tucked it into Lisa's thick hair. She put her head on his shoulder, and they continued their quiet, dreamy walk along the fragrant path.

The path ended and they stood on the sandy shore of Coco Bay. Lisa noticed that the few houses in the area seemed deserted, yet she heard voices and loud laughter. Then she saw a group of people sitting on a small dock. She thought they were watching the brilliant tropical sunset—until she heard a familiar laugh.

"Jessica," she said.

"Yeah. Let's get out of here," said Michael as he pulled Lisa back to the path.

Jessica came running after them. "Michael," she called, "I thought that was you."

She held a glassful of amber liquid in her hands and sipped from it as she stood.

"Come join us, huh?"

"Thanks, but no thanks," said Michael.

"Aw, c'mon. We're havin' fun."

"Jessica, you're crazy," Michael said sharply. "What're you drinking? And who are those kids?"

"Oh, they're just some boys Peter and I met around the marina. They've got this great rum and papaya juice stuff. You oughta try some."

"Do your aunt and uncle know you're here?"

"Nah, what they don't know won't hurt them."

Lisa stared as Jessica swayed and tried to keep her balance. "Jessica, you don't even know those boys—they might get you in all sorts of trouble."

Michael said: "You aren't safe with a gang of strangers like that—especially when you're not quite sober. C'mon, Jessica, come back with us and—"

"Geez, Michael," said Jessica, "you sound like your goody-goody girl friend. Bug off, you two, and leave me alone."

"Wow, what a mess," said Lisa as she and Michael walked back to the club.

"Yeah, it is. But it's not our problem now. She won't listen to us, so we'll just have to forget it."

Michael got his guitar from the dinghy and he and Lisa went into the small club. It was crowded—young people, older people, white, black, some wearing shorts, some dressed up. Lisa and Michael sat a small wooden table and sipped pineapple juice and coconut milk frappés.

The rooms decorations intrigued Lisa. Colorful yacht club burgees from everywhere hung on the walls. She recognized the swallow-tailed pennant of her dad's yacht club in Boston. Music filled the room. The crowd clapped and stomped and sang. A few couples danced, but Lisa realized that, even if her ankle were healed, there wouldn't be room for one more couple on the tiny dance floor.

Michael strummed on his guitar. He offered her the instrument. She played along with the other musicians. One of the band members motioned her to the small stage. She hesitated, but Michael urged her to go on.

She sat on the stage edge, the skirt of her vividly striped dress fell in soft folds across her legs. Her gleaming long hair fell forward as she played a medley of John Lennon songs. When Lisa strummed and sang "All we are saying is give peace a chance," the crowd joined her and a spirit of harmony filled the room.

Michael moved to her side. He gently pushed her hair off her face and tucked the hibiscus securely in place. He smiled at her as he took his guitar and softly played and sang "Black, black is the color of my true love's hair—"

Lisa felt she had never known such happiness.

7

Lisa didn't need an alarm to awaken her in the morning. The three men clopped around the deck above her cabin. Through the open hatch above her head she heard the Skipper barking orders. Just like Captain Bligh in *Mutiny on the Bounty*, she thought.

When she finally climbed topside, the Skipper was at the wheel and her dad and Michael were hoisting the huge white sails. The little dinghy nestled close to the stern and it bobbed up and down on the wavelets.

"Take the helm, will you, Lisa?" asked the Skipper. "I'll give them a hand with the sails."

Lisa held the large wheel gently and felt

Dream Weaver respond to the brisk southwest wind that billowed the sails and carried the boat swiftly through the green water.

"I'd better take over now," said the Skipper. "Our next course is tricky—we've got to work our way out there," he pointed to the rocky tip of a cay and to the ocean beyond.

"How come we're going out in the ocean? It sure looks wild," she said to Michael.

"It's just for a coupla miles. This water's too shallow for our boat." He showed her on the chart how they'd go around Whale Cay into the Atlantic, and then head back into the sheltered water on the protected side of the cays.

Lisa watched the big waves hit the reefs, sending spray flying so that it looked like falling white rain. "Is it only thirty feet deep here? The navy-blue water looks deeper than that," she said as she studied the chart.

"That's thirty fathoms—at six feet a fathom," Michael explained.

In no time *Dream Weaver* was back in the calm waters that paralleled the shoreline.

"There's Great Guana Cay," Michael told her. "We're going to tie up there and have lunch at the Guana Harbour Club. Maybe we can go for a swim—the beach on the ocean side is sensational."

After a meal of turtle soup, broiled grouper

and blueberry pie with guava ice cream, Michael and Lisa were ready to hit the beach. But The Fathers weren't.

"The wind's dropped to nothing," said the Skipper. "Might as well turn on the iron lung and not bother with the sails. We want to get to Marsh Harbour before sunset."

Lisa knew that real sailors like her dad and the Skipper resented using engines. "You're supposed to sail a sailboat, not drive it," her dad always said.

"But I thought we were going the long way—by Water Cay. I wanted Lisa to see it," Michael said.

"We are, but we've got to get moving."

"What's at Water Cay?" asked Lisa.

"Did you ever see the movie *Day of the Dolphins*?" asked Michael.

"Oh, sure, a coupla times on TV. It was super."

"They trained the dolphins and shot the movie at Water Cay. The whole area is still full of tame dolphins. You'll be able to get some keen pictures around there."

"Thanks, Michael, for reminding me about pictures. I don't want to ever forget a minute of this trip."

Dream Weaver's engine sounded sick, even to Lisa's untrained ears—it coughed, sputtered and then stopped. As the Skipper uttered a few well-chosen words about the situation, Lisa looked at Michael to see if he was as concerned as his pop.

"We're in an awful mess," he told her. "No wind, no engine and a strong current pushing us toward a rocky cay."

"What happens now?"

"Just stay calm, pop'll tell us what to do."

Lisa's dad went forward and dropped a large anchor into the water.

"We'll need a second anchor to hold us in this current," said the Skipper. "Lisa, put the swim ladder over the side. Michael, pull the dinghy alongside and row it up to the bow." As Lisa and Michael got into action, Lisa's dad brought out another anchor on a heavy chain. He handed it to Michael who stowed it in the dinghy. The bigger end of the chain was secured to *Dream Weaver*'s bow. Michael rowed the little boat away from the large one as Lisa played out the chain over the dinghy's stern. Then Michael dropped the anchor about fifty feet opposite the first one.

"That should do it, but you'd better check both anchors," shouted the Skipper.

Michael dived into the clear shallow water. Lisa watched as he tugged on both anchors and made sure they were securely set.

The Fathers went to the engine room to work on the dead diesel engine.

"You've had your swim," Lisa said to Michael. "Is it okay if I go in now?"

"Sure."

"Ouch," she said as she neared the bottom of the ladder.

"What's the matter?"

"Scraped my foot on a rough spot on the last rung."

"You'll live, won't ya?"

"Yeah." As Lisa swam away from the boat she thought how much she loved Michael's teasing and easy-going attitude.

She cavorted in the translucent ripples and waved gaily to Michael who watched her from *Dream Weaver*. As she romped in the warm water she saw Michael beckoning her and calling out something. She floated lazily toward the boat.

"Lisa, come back. Hurry." He repeated his urging twice before she understood him clearly. She turned on her stomach to swim to him when she saw a fin gliding toward her through the water. How great, she thought, a trained dolphin had come to play with her. She saw that Michael had moved to *Dream Weaver*'s stern.

He had a gun in his hands! And in a few seconds she heard three sharp cracks from the rifle and three bullets hit the water about six feet from her. She swam as fast as she could toward the boat. She panicked when she realized she was fighting the current and couldn't make much progress. Her ankle hurt and she could barely kick her left leg.

The Fathers came to the cockpit just as Michael was poised to dive in.

"No, Michael," Lisa's dad yelled. "There may be more around. Quick, tie a line around a boat cushion, heave it to her and tow her in."

The three men lifted a scared Lisa into the cockpit. "Why did you shoot? Wasn't it a dolphin?" she asked when she caught her breath.

"A small shark, but still dangerous," said Michael. "I was watching you and just happened to see the thing heading for you—must have been attracted by the blood from the cut on your leg."

"It's not much more than a scratch, it was hardly bleeding."

"Doesn't take much to draw a shark," Michael told her.

Lisa shivered. She pictured the sharks in *Jaws* and remembered how revolted she was by that movie. She also recalled how upset she'd been at the mention of guns aboard the boat. She wanted to hug Michael and thank him for saving her from a shark bite. But her dad had noticed her shivering and insisted that she take a warm shower, bundle up in a blanket and take a nap.

She heard the Skipper tell the others they'd have to stay anchored where they were. The engine job would take a couple more hours and by then it'd be too dark to go anywhere else.

The Fathers were still busy in the engine room when Lisa awoke. She and Michael sat in the cockpit and watched the salmon-pink sunset over the nearby tiny cay. They heard a plane overhead, but no other sounds broke the silence of the evening.

"Where are we?" asked Lisa. "It sure is lonely out here."

"According to the chart, that's privately owned land—Foot's Cay. The house looks deserted, doesn't it?"

"The whole place looks spooky," said Lisa as she watched the sun's afterglow turn to eerie darkness.

"Yeah, it is. You hungry?"

"Not very. We had a huge lunch."

"Let's fix some BLT's in pita bread. We'll use up the lettuce and tomatoes we have and get more in Marsh Harbour—if we ever get there."

"Michael, don't talk like that. I'm still shook up from this afternoon."

"Wow, what a trip *that* was."

"I'll never forget how you saved my life, Michael."

"Aw, Lisa, it was no big deal. I doubt if the shark would have eaten more than an arm or leg."

During supper the Skipper said, "I don't like this anchorage much. We're off the regular course to anywhere. It's pitch black and we're just sitting here, open to anyone who comes along."

"We have more work to do on the engine," the Skipper continued. "Lisa, you turn on lots of lights below. Michael, go flip on the mast light and the spreader light—at least no one will run into us if we're all lit up. And I want both of you to stand watch in the cockpit. Understood?"

"Aye, aye, Sir," they both answered.

"And," he went on, "if you hear or see anything suspicious—anything at all—get out of sight. Get on the cockpit sole and crawl to the companionway and call me—quietly."

That sounded ominous to Lisa. She figured she'd had all the excitement she needed for one day.

Michael and Lisa sat outside in the chilly evening and watched the stars. Lisa repeated the rhyme, "Star light, star bright, I wish I may, I wish I might have the—"

Before she got her wish, she and Michael jumped as they heard a quick hissing sound. The boat's generator had stopped running. The lights went out—including those outside on the mast and spreader that served as anchor lights.

Lisa knew from the Skipper's usual string of oaths that something had happened in the engine room.

"*All* the lights are out, Skipper," she called.

"Probably blew the main circuit breaker. Take a look at it, Michael. But first get me the large flashlight. We'll need it down here so we can see to get this blasted engine together again. Then dig out that kerosene anchor light and get it raised as fast as you can."

"This'll take five or ten minutes," Michael told Lisa. He patted her arm reassuringly. "Don't be scared, but remember to keep a close watch for anything—"

"Oh, Michael, please—don't spook me anymore. Anyhow, all I hear is another plane."

Lisa sat alone in the cockpit. She was astonished at how many more stars there seemed to be when no lights diluted the blackness of the night. "I wish I may, I wish I might have the wish I wish tonight," she said softly. She drew Michael's shirt more closely around her and lost herself in idle, pleasant thoughts about him and their growing friendship.

Her reverie was interrupted by a faint sound in the distance. Must be fish jumping, she thought. She slid along the cockpit seat toward the stern of the boat, and peered aft into the darkness. She saw the ghost of something moving toward *Dream Weaver*.

She got on her hands and knees and crawled to the companionway hatch. "Skipper," she called softly, "there's something behind us—maybe a boat."

"Keep out of sight and get down here!" he told Lisa. "Michael, where are you? Quick, go to the engine room and douse the flashlight—then you and Lisa stay together, someplace out of sight."

Michael put a protective arm around Lisa as they watched her dad and the Skipper each grab a gun and stand side by side on the narrow ladder. They climbed only high enough so they could search the darkness of the cockpit and the surrounding water.

Suddenly *Dream Weaver* was flooded in the brilliance of huge searchlights. Lisa and Michael peeped through the salon window and saw a gray cutter pull alongside. Large black initials—BASRA—were painted on the bow of the intruding boat.

"Bahamas Air Sea Rescue Auxiliary,"

whispered Michael. "Sorta like our Coast Guard. Wonder what they want?"

Two uniformed men, armed with rifles stood on the deck of the BASRA boat. "Ahoy, Captain, prepare to be boarded for search."

Lisa watched her dad and the Skipper go topside, guns in hand.

"Identify yourself," said the Skipper.

"Basra," said one of the men. Lisa noticed that he pronounced the initials on his boat like a word. "We have authority from the Seventh District United States Coast Guard to search any suspicious American vessel."

"Why is my vessel suspicious?" asked the Skipper.

"One of our planes spotted you in this isolated spot at sunset, and later without lights. *That's* suspicious."

"One of you may come aboard and show me official identification," said the Skipper. He raised his rifle to waist height as the Bahamian stepped onto *Dream Weaver*'s deck. Michael and Lisa had moved to the open hatch so they could look up and see what was going on. The man handed the Skipper an ID card.

"How do I know this is authentic identification?" said the Skipper.

"We have run a complete customs check on you." The BASRA man then detailed all the information *Dream Weaver*'s crew had given the inspectors at West End, including the serial numbers of the guns the Skipper and Lisa's dad still held.

The Fathers looked at each other questioningly. Lisa saw her dad shrug his shoulders and slowly nod his head yes.

"You may search below, but leave your rifle topside. My friend will accompany you," said the Skipper.

"He must disarm also," the man insisted.

Lisa's dad and the searcher came below. "Turn on some lights," the man said to Michael and Lisa.

Michael explained about the lights and the engine trouble. The man listened attentively while he snooped around the salon, galley and dinette.

It didn't seem to Lisa that he was making much of a search.

"Exactly what're you looking for?" she asked politely.

"Drugs—marijuana, heroin and the like."

"Oh, but we told them at customs we didn't have any drugs."

"Well, Miss, everyone says that; but not everyone tells the truth. We're making spot searches of United States boats, especially those from southern Florida."

"And *Dream Weaver*'s from Fort Lauderdale," said Lisa.

"Right. We're working closely with your Coast Guard to stop pleasure boats from making drug pickups in the Bahamas, and from bringing drugs into our country."

"But we told the truth. We don't have anything illegal aboard."

"I believe you." He turned to Lisa's dad, "We'll call off the search now, let's go topside."

The man told his companion that *Dream Weaver* was okay. He apologized to the Skipper and urged him to show some sort of identifying light in the dark night. The second BASRA man said he was an electrician and he offered to take a look at the wiring or whatever the Skipper thought was wrong with the boat's power system.

"We could use an expert," said Lisa's dad. "We've been working on the engine almost all day and now this—"

"And, besides," said Lisa, "everything in our freezer will melt."

"Lisa," said the Skipper, "why don't you and Michael fire up the propane stove and make a pot of coffee for us? Maybe these men would like a sandwich or something."

"Sure would," said one of them. "We left Hope Town before supper and it'll be awhile before we get back." His companion found what was wrong with the wiring and had it fixed in a few minutes. The group sat in the softly lit salon and thanked Lisa for the coffee and sandwiches she served them.

"Is Basra still a volunteer group?" the Skipper asked.

"Yes, Sir. The government pays for our fuel, but the boats and planes are privately owned. We're supported by memberships and donations. Someday we'll have a regular Coast Guard similar to yours, but for now we do the best we can."

"And from all I've heard, you do a great job. We'd like to donate something to your group," said the Skipper. He and Lisa's dad gave the two men some money. "Thank you very much, Sirs. It will be put to good use."

As the men prepared to leave *Dream Weaver* one of them asked Lisa if she'd been to Hope Town yet.

"No, but we'll be there in a few days."

He told her some good places to shop in his village and said he hoped she'd enjoy her visit there.

"What a day," said the Skipper after the boat departed. "Let's all hit the sack."

Lisa draped Michael's shirt over her pajamas and lay in her bunk and tried to read herself to sleep.

"Lisa, are you still awake?" her dad called softly.

"Yeah, come on in, Dad."

"You've had quite a day, Pet. Are you okay?"

"Oh, sure—I guess so."

"Something's bothering you, isn't it? Anything you want to tell me about, Pet?"

"No, it's really nothing."

"Is it . . . maybe Michael?"

"Oh, no, Dad, it certainly isn't Michael! I was just thinking about something, but I'm not sure I should tell you about it."

"What?"

Lisa remained silent. Her dad fixed his gaze on the gold pine cone pin she wore on the collar of Michael's shirt. Lisa knew his glance was meant to remind her of their pact to share their problems.

"Listen," she finally said, "I don't want to tell you this because it's none of my business. But I think somebody should know about Jessica."

And she told him how she and Michael had seen Jessica with a group of strangers and how Jessica had had too much to drink.

"You were right to tell me, Lisa. Jessica's aunt and uncle should know what she's been doing. Do you know where they went from Green Turtle?"

"That nice boy with them, David, said they were going to Man-O-War."

"Okay. I'll take care of it, don't let it bother you anymore. Go to sleep now, Pet."

8

"We're going to Man-O-War today, not Marsh Harbour," Michael told Lisa at breakfast.

"Yeah, I know."

"D'ya know why?"

"Yep. I decided I had to tell my dad about Jessica being drunk."

"You told *your* dad? When?"

"Last night—after you went to bed."

"Lisa, that's when I told *my* pop about it."

"Oh, Michael, I didn't think you were that concerned about it."

"Well, I was. It's really dangerous to get too friendly with strangers around a marina. Those guys could even be hijackers for all we know. And Jessica could have gotten into a bad scene with that group. Somebody had to be told about her behavior."

"I'm with you. But Jessica's going to be furious!"

"That's her problem, not ours."

Dream Weaver entered the narrow harbor at Man-O-War, but Lisa scarcely noticed the picturesque settlement as she scanned the anchorage for *Happy Daze*. The big houseboat wasn't there.

The Fathers, Michael and Lisa piled into their dinghy and rowed ashore for lunch at the only restaurant in town—*Dock 'N Dine*. As soon as the Fathers finished their conch fritters they went off to one of the town's boatyards to get spare parts for the engine. Lisa and Michael polished off their meal with coconut pie and ice cream.

They walked around the narrow streets and admired the brightly painted wooden houses. Lobster-pot markers and fishnet balls hanging from the trees decorated most of the tiny homes. Many had religious mottoes painted above their doorways. Large conch shells with their tulip-shaped pink openings outlined yards and walkways. Everywhere Lisa looked she saw flowers. The fragrance of Easter lilies, alamanda and frangapani filled the air. Churches of all sizes were everywhere. Lisa noticed no cars—just bikes and motorcycles.

Michael plucked a yellow alamanda blossom and tucked it in Lisa's dark hair. She smiled her thanks and commented, "The Alburys practically own this town, don't they?"

"Yeah, they're into everything. A couple of boatyards, grocery store, a ferry to the other cays, a yacht dock—and the cemetery's full of their relatives. Let's walk up there."

As they left the waterfront Lisa looked around to be sure *Happy Daze* hadn't arrived. Michael watched her and she realized he understood what she was doing.

He gave her hand a reassuring squeeze. "Relax, Lisa, The Fathers are gonna take care of everything. Don't let Jessica's problem spoil your fun."

They climbed up through a palm-lined picnic grove to the cemetery. Lisa couldn't believe she'd find a cemetery beautiful! All the graves were bedecked with fresh flowers and many were rimmed with large shells. A modestly dressed woman looked up from the plot she was tending and greeted Michael and Lisa. She admired Lisa's cane and gave the couple some graceful conch shells and a paper bag full of pears from an over-hanging tree.

"And here's a coconut," she said to Lisa. "Your boyfriend can crack it and you drink the milk out of the shell, then eat chunks of the coconut meat." Lisa's heart jumped at the thought of Michael as her boyfriend, but she tried not to let him see how delighted she was.

"Their pears are our avocados," she said to Michael as they headed down toward the ocean beach. "And have you noticed, they say conk, they don't pronounce it the way it's spelled."

Still thinking of the woman at the cemetery, Michael said, "She liked you. Probably because you're wearing a skirt. The folks here are very conservative. I can imagine how they'll glare at Jessica if she walks around here in her usual outfits."

Lisa gasped at her first glimpse of the Atlantic and its shoreline. "What a sight," she exclaimed. Huge and menacing breakers pounded the reef. Inside the rocky barrier the turquoise water was flat and the sand didn't even have a footprint on it.

"Would you believe," said Michael, "that you can dive behind that reef and see the wreck of the South's battleship, *Adirondack*— she sank in 1860. She's lying on her side in about twenty feet of water, you can even see her cannon."

"You're a good teacher, Michael. Is that what you want to be?"

"Nah, couldn't afford it! I'm gonna get into aeronautical engineering—space stuff."

"Hey, maybe someday I'll be programming your stuff into a computer," Lisa said.

"Wow, it's time to meet The Fathers," Michael said.

They walked back down the hill to the docks. Lisa noticed there was still no sign of *Happy Daze* in the harbor.

"About time you got here," the Skipper said. He and Lisa's dad sat in front of *Dock 'N Dine* on a bench with a sign over it that read, "Gabby Bench, Where the Elite Meet."

"Lisa," her dad said, "the only way I'm going to get you to call your mother is lead you by the hand to a phone."

"I've tried a couple of times, but she's never home."

"The telephone's in the post office next to the school," Michael said. "And it's only open certain hours," the Skipper added.

Other tourists were in line for the phone and Lisa was told to come back in a half hour. During that time they discovered Albury's Sail Loft. The Fathers were interested in the boat sails that were made there. But Lisa dragged Michael to the end of the shop where two women sewed and sold canvas accessories.

"I've got to have one of these hats," Lisa said. She tried on a flat-topped hat with a wide brim that could be set any which way. She decided on a white one and convinced Michael to get one like it. The Skipper decided that he and each of his crew needed a zippered sailing jacket, and he bought one apiece. He was told that it wouldn't take too long for *Dream Weaver* to be embroidered in navy blue on back of the jackets. The Skipper and Michael waited for that to be done while Lisa and her dad went to the phone office.

The call to New Hampshire went through quickly—but the conversation didn't. Lisa was too intent on what her mom was saying to notice that her dad, Michael and the Skipper were now pacing impatiently outside the phone booth.

"She wants me to come home next week," Lisa said when she finally joined them.

Angrily, her dad said, "Why? You're supposed to be with me a month—not three weeks."

"Gee, Lisa," said Michael, "you won't be able to sail back with us—you'll have to fly."

Lisa took her dad's hand. "Mom's getting married."

She noticed the tightened expression around his mouth. "That's nice," he said, flatly. "Who's the lucky guy?"

"Lewis Barnett, a history prof at Dexter."

Lisa sensed that her dad was too stunned to talk about it right then, so she didn't say anything else. She clung to his hand as though she could help him sort out his emotions.

"Is he the guy you were going to work for this summer?" Michael asked.

Lisa wished Michael would let the subject drop. "Yeah, he's the one," she said.

"Gee, now that he'll be your stepfather maybe he won't even pay you."

Lisa felt her dad's hand clasp hers more firmly.

"My stepfather!" she said. "I don't need a stepfather—I've got a perfectly super father right here. As far as I'm concerned he'll be . . . he'll just be my mother's husband."

Lisa noticed the compassionate look that passed from the Skipper to her dad. She imagined that the two old friends were both thinking of when the Skipper's wife got married again. She wished Michael knew more about that situation. It was awful, she thought, that he didn't even know his mother.

"What d'ya suppose you'll call this guy?" Michael asked.

"Who knows? He's always been Professor Barnett to me."

"You can't call him that if you're living in his house."

"He's going to live in our house. I'll just call him 'you' or maybe 'Barney,' like my mom does."

"But—"

"That's enough, Michael," the Skipper said. "They'll want to discuss this later—alone."

Back aboard *Dream Weaver*, the Skipper set the cribbage board on the dinette table and challenged Michael to a game.

"How do you feel about your mother's news, Lisa?" her dad asked as they sat together on the cozy couch in the salon.

"It's okay with me."

"I mean, do you like him—Lewis Barnett?"

"Yeah, he's a pretty nice guy."

"Has your mother known him long?"

"Ever since we left you and moved to Dexter. Of course, I never knew they . . . well, ya know, I never thought of them *that* way— married and all, I mean."

Her dad laughed heartily. "I get what you mean! I remember when I was young I could never think of my parents 'that way.'"

"Gee, you don't suppose they'll have a baby, do ya?"

"I guess it's possible—wouldn't you like that?"

"Yeech! My best friend's mom just had a baby and all she does is babysit for free—my friend, I mean."

"What's the professor like?"

"He's nice. He and mom go to concerts and stuff like that. When he comes over to the house they play Scrabble and listen to good music—that's what they call it, anyhow. He uses big words, and he and mom talk a lot about books."

"Sounds as though he and your mother make a good pair."

"I never paid much attention to their . . . to their relationship. But, yes, they do make a good pair. I think they'll be great together. Mom seemed different already, she's changing in some way."

"What do you mean?"

"I don't know how to say it—she didn't sound like a mother, she talked to me like a person, not like a kid."

"Maybe you heard her differently—you're changing, too, you know."

"Yeah, I guess you're right."

"You talked a long time. What else did she have to say?"

"Oh, they're getting married in the school chapel and she wants me to buy a pretty dress when I get home. I told her you bought me a dreamy one that'd be perfect for a wedding. And, oh yeah, she said she arranged for me to stay with a friend while she's on her honeymoon—they're going to New York for a week. Some honeymoon!"

"Did she say anything about me?"

"Just asked how we were getting along—I told her great, we were good pals. She said she was glad to hear that."

Lisa pushed back her glasses and looked intently at him. "Dad, you're not unhappy about mom's getting married, are you? You're not still in love with her or anything like that?"

"Oh, Pet, you and your imagination! No, I'm not unhappy about it. As a matter of fact, I'm very happy for her. He's probably more her type than I was. And no, I'm not still in love with her. Even though people are apart, they still care about each other and want the best of everything for them."

It was then that Lisa realized how soon she and Michael would be parted and an empty, lonesome little ache settled in her stomach.

"I'm sure," her dad continued, "everything will work out fine at home for you, too. And, of course, I'll continue to send money enough for your needs. And I'm going to send you a check every month so you'll have more spending money than your mom seems to give you."

"Hey, that'll be great—I'm always broke. And, you know, I won't feel like I have to keep mom company on holidays and weekends now—so maybe I can get down to see you more."

"That suits me!" He hugged her hard. "Oh, Pet, I love you so very, very much."

Lisa's loving look at him was filled with emotion. She felt all good and warm inside— the way she did when she came home on a freezing cold day and drank a cup of hot chocolate.

"Michael," she heard the Skipper say as he entered the salon, "cribbage is for old salts like me. It'll be a long time before you can beat me at my own game."

"Guess I'll have to teach Lisa—maybe I can beat her."

Lisa noticed that her dad had looked out the window and had nodded at the Skipper.

"Michael, we're going out with the dinghy for awhile," his pop said. "And when we get back I want you and Lisa to dink over to the dump and get rid of all the garbage bags in the engine room."

Lisa knew, even before she looked outside, that *Happy Daze* had arrived and that was where The Fathers were going.

Michael tried to teach her to play cribbage, but she was too preoccupied to concentrate on all those "fifteens" and "thirty-ones" and "goes."

"What's the matter, Lisa, too complicated for you?"

"Nah, just thinking about other things."

"You still worried about Jessica?"

"Yeah, that's part of it."

"Are ya upset about your mom?"

"Oh, no, that's super news. Now she'll have someone to take care of besides me. Maybe she'll let me grow up by myself."

"Seems you're doing a lot of that already. Something's bugging you—what's the matter?"

"I keep thinking that I have to leave you a whole week earlier—we don't have much time left to be together."

"Well, don't get all bent out of shape about it—the trip home'll be pretty boring anyway."

Lisa couldn't believe that any time she spent with Michael would be boring. It seemed that he couldn't care less about spending fewer days with her.

"Don't look so sad, Lisa. Pop thinks I should fly home with you. Would that be okay?"

"That's just wonderful! All the way to Boston? That's where my mom will meet me."

"Well, no, to Miami—but I'll put you on your flight to Boston."

"Are you sure all I'll miss is the sail back to Florida?"

"Yeah. The Fathers will go back to West End the way we came—and you've seen most of that. Heck, Lisa, we still have almost a week."

"Will we go to Marsh Harbour?"

"Sure—that's where the plane leaves from, anyhow. And we'll get to Hope Town, too. We'll talk to pop when he gets back and—"

"I wonder if they'll tell us what happened on *Happy Daze*? I guess there's no way Jessica won't know we told on her."

"I guess not—and I don't care all that much. C'mon, we'd better get the garbage bags on deck. The Fathers'll be back soon."

"Where do we have to go?"

"The town dump at the end of the harbor. If this breeze holds up, let's sail the dinghy down there."

"Sounds like more fun than rowing it."

The Fathers reported to Michael and Lisa that Jessica's relatives were upset over her behavior and they appreciated being told about it. Lisa's eyebrows asked her dad a question. "No," he said, "we didn't see Jessica. Your friend David was there, and he assured us that he didn't know anything about it. He seems like a nice kid."

"Yeah," she said. "He's going to Yale."

Surrounded by three heavy green trash bags, two oars, two boat cushions and a bailing bucket, Michael and Lisa stuffed themselves into the dinghy. They rigged the small triangular sail to the slim mast and its lightweight wooden boom.

The little boat rose and fell gently as it topped the wavelets. Occasionally, the greenish water slapped against the side and sent light spray over the edge. The afternoon breeze was light and steady, but Lisa and Michael made slow progress down the harbor.

"I think we're slightly overloaded," she said.

"We're sure getting nowhere fast. After we get rid of this junk we'll get in a little sailing," Michael said.

They sat side by side on the tiny seat. Michael gently stroked Lisa's dark head. "Your hair looks so pretty blowing in the breeze. That's the first thing I noticed about you. I'll always remember—"

His words were lost in the roar of a motorboat racing toward them. Its wake created large swells that made the anchored boats bounce and sway.

Lisa knew exactly who was in that boat—even before she saw Jessica's blonde hair flying behind her. The large Boston Whaler approached the small dinghy and circled around and around it—each circle churning the surrounding water.

Jessica stood at the wheel of her buzzing boat. Angrily, she screeched at Lisa and Michael. "You finks! You lousy jerks! What a pair of tattletales you are! I hate both of you."

Round and round she went; her boat roughed up the water and made it impossible for Michael and Lisa to control their dinghy. The last pass of Jessica's boat was too much for the smaller one—over it went! And Jessica roared back up the harbor.

Lisa and Michael splashed into the water. Garbage bags bobbed in the turbulence. Oars and cushions floated off in every direction. The little dinghy lay on its side, water filled its sail. Michael and Lisa hung onto the boat's side and struggled to loosen the sail from its rigging. They needed to dump the water from the sail so they could pull the boat right side up.

Once they managed that, Michael boosted Lisa aboard and told her to cup her hands and start bailing out as much water as she could. He swam to the debris and rescued the bailing bucket, oars and cushions.

"I'll grab the garbage bags and tow them over to the dock," he told her. "You keep bailing, then row over to me."

At last the boat was shipshape, and the little sail was again attached to the mast and boom.

Lisa's face was pink with anger. "My glasses! They fell off when I hit the water. Oh, what'll I do?"

"Gosh, I dunno. I can dive around where we went over, but the bottom's all grassy—I can't promise you I'll find them."

Lisa sat in the dinghy and watched Michael make numerous futile dives.

She heard the soft purr of an engine and turned to see what boat approached them. She didn't need her glasses to see that it was Jessica!

Jessica idled her craft alongside Lisa in the small dinghy. Michael surfaced and quickly hoisted his body into his boat and stood behind Lisa. They listened with amazement as Jessica asked sweetly, "Are y'all okay?" before gunning her motor, leaving behind her a foamy wake.

9

Kids!" said the Skipper when the bedraggled pair related their experience with Jessica. "You never know what they'll do next!"

"But my glasses! What'll I do?" Lisa asked. Somehow she felt her father had not taken in the situation.

"Don't you have a spare pair?" her dad asked.

"Yes, but they're at home."

Her dad frowned. "Didn't your mother ever tell you to always take a spare?" he asked crossly.

"There's an eye doctor in the clinic in Marsh Harbour," Michael said. "I got some sunglasses from him last year."

"I doubt that he grinds lenses, probably sends off to someplace in Florida to have them done," she heard her dad say.

"Wait a minute," said the Skipper, "I've got an idea. A friend of mine, Jim White, owns a string of vision centers. You know who I mean, Michael—your friend Christine's father."

"Yeah, I know who you mean," Michael answered.

"I could call Jim and get the doc in Marsh Harbour to talk to him, too. I'm sure Jim could do a rush job on some fancy glasses for Lisa. He could put them on a plane and she'd have them in a few days."

"Sounds like a lot of trouble to me," Lisa's dad said.

"Not as much trouble as we'll have if that young lady can't see," the Skipper said.

"I think we should try the guy in Marsh Harbour," Michael said.

"Okay," said Lisa's dad.

"If we leave right now we can make Marsh Harbour in an hour or so, way before dark. Michael," ordered his pop, "get on the CB and ask Conch Inn to save us a spot in the marina —and make a dinner reservation.

"We'll fill our water tanks there and top off the fuel. And," the Skipper continued, "the boat and dinghy need a good hosing down.

You and Lisa can do that at dockside tomorrow."

"I'll call Jim tonight," he went on. "We'd better know for sure this can be done. Do you want to talk to Christine, Michael?"

"Aw, c'mon, Pop, lay off that now, will ya?" Michael's tone was one of disgust. Lisa wondered who Christine was. She decided she might ask Michael later when they were alone. Could it be his girl friend?

Since they were going out to dinner at Marsh Harbour, Lisa wore her pink jeans outfit. With a little shoving she'd been able to get her injured foot into a pink espadrille. Like Cinderella, she thought, as she entered the galley and saw Michael, her Prince Charming.

"You look great," he said. "We're going to eat in a neat place and you'll be the prettiest girl there."

She batted her huge eyes at him, "Thanks." Lisa loved not wearing glasses. With them on, her long lashes kind of folded back against the lenses. Without them, she could flutter her lashes so they looked like wind blowing on a feather.

She noticed Michael, head cocked to one side, staring at her as though getting ready to paint or, maybe, frame a picture of her head.

"Why don't you get contacts, Lisa?"

"I've thought about it, but my mom didn't think it was such a great idea. She said I'd always lose them."

"Nah, once you get used to 'em there's not much chance of losing them. Besides, your mom's not here, your dad's in charge now."

Her dark eyes opened wide in contemplation of such mutiny and they sparkled with anticipation.

"You'd love 'em," he said. "Your glasses're always sliding down your nose and that must be a nuisance."

"Is it ever! I can never get them to fit right. When they stay on my nose they hurt behind my ears."

"I think soft contacts would do something for you—give you more self-confidence, let you throw back your head and laugh—ya know what I'm trying to say?"

"Would you like me better without glasses, Michael?"

"I'd like you anyway, Lisa. The point is I think you'd like yourself better," he said.

"D'ya suppose I could get them quickly?"

"Probably even faster than glasses. All the different strength lenses are numbered. The eye doctor would only have to call pop's friend and tell him what numbers to send for you."

"How would I ever learn to put them in? It's tricky, isn't it?"

"I could teach you. I've watched a friend of mine pop hers in and out a million times."

"Christine?" she blushed. But curiosity overcame her embarrassment. "Is she your girl friend?"

"Nah, not really. I don't have a steady. I'm too busy to get that involved."

"What d'ya do with yourself, besides school, I mean."

"I'm into flying lessons, ground school, anyhow. And a science club, an astronomy club—"

"I guess you are too busy for girls!"

"Well—I didn't mean *that* exactly."

The Skipper called them to come topside and get to work.

"Get some docking lines ready, Michael," he ordered. "We'll need two bows and two sterns. And, Lisa, you reach down into that lazarette and get the two biggest fenders."

She leaned into the deep storage bin to find the round rubber bumpers. As she did this she realized if she'd been wearing her glases, they'd have fallen off by now, or at least have slipped to the end of her nose.

"Dad? What would ya think about my getting contacts instead of glasses?"

"Great idea! If you don't lose too many of them."

Yes, she thought, he's being a real father-mother, just as he'd promised.

The Skipper eased *Dream Weaver* between two sets of high yellow pilings. Michael expertly tossed a rope loop on one, her dad did the other one. Lisa threw the bow lines to the dockmaster. She was glad he caught them so easily because she could hardly see his outstretched arm.

A short time later, when all were seated in the Conch Inn's attractive dining room, Lisa didn't want anyone to know she couldn't read the menu so she said she'd just have a hamburger.

"But this place is famous for its cracked conch. You should try it," her dad said. "If you want a hamburger you can get one in the Conch Crawl later on."

"What's that?" she asked.

"Kind of a snack bar near the swimming pool," Michael said. "While we're waiting for dinner is it okay if I go over there and see if we've got any mail?" Michael asked his pop.

"I hope you gave everyone the Conch Inn as a mailing address, Lisa," said the Skipper.

"Sure did. Is it a real post office?"

"Nothing like that," he laughed. "There's a clothesline strung along the bar and letters for yachts are clipped on it with wooden clothespins."

Lisa looked around the wicker and chintz room with its old-fashioned fans purring overhead. The setting sun glared through large picture windows and blinded her already hazy eyes. The Skipper went to call his friend about Lisa's contacts while they waited to be served.

"The dish we've ordered tonight is conch meat pounded tissue thin, rolled in butter and deep fried," her dad said.

"Sounds delicious. I wish they'd hurry, I'm starved."

"Mailman," called Michael as he returned with a handful of envelopes. The Fathers' mail looked official and legal. Lisa had a letter from her mom and two from her best friend. She would have to wait until she got glasses or contacts before she could read them. When, she wondered, would Michael read the several letters he furtively stuck in his pocket? Was one from Christine? Or worse, were they all from her?

"Everything's arranged," the Skipper reported as he sat down to enjoy his meal. "Jim'll put the contacts on a plane as soon as Doctor Jones calls in Lisa's prescription. I called the doc at home and he'll see Lisa at ten in the morning."

Michael guided Lisa to Dr. Jones' office the next day.

"The only problem you'll have with contacts," he told Lisa, "is losing a lens in your thick eyelashes. I'll let you know as soon as the package gets to the airport. Then come see me again and we'll get you fixed up."

"Honestly, Lisa, you're silly to feel self-conscious about wearing glasses," Michael said when they reached the street again. "You'll have to wear them once in awhile even after you've got the contacts, to give your eyes a rest."

"They look so crummy," she said.

"Yeah, well, I think how you look isn't as important as how you see."

Lisa laughed. "You're right—it *is* kinda childish and vain," she admitted. She felt light-headed and happy to be able to say something like that to Michael.

He took her arm. "Come on, we've gotta get the stuff out of the laundromat now. The Fathers said we'd leave for Hope Town about thirteen hundred."

Shortly after one o'clock *Dream Weaver* was underway. Lisa and Michael had barely finished eating an unhealthy lunch of Bahamian bread—hot, doughy and dripping with rich butter—when the Skipper yelled for Michael to come topside and pick up a mooring in the harbor.

Hope Town's famous candy-striped lighthouse, perched on a hilltop, overlooked the anchorage. Across the water, pastel-hued houses tumbled down to the palm and flower covered shores. Lisa wondered which houses belonged to the Basra men. She remembered the shops they'd recommended and urged Michael to hurry with his letter writing and take her ashore.

"D'ya mind going in alone?" he asked. He pointed out the Government Dock where she could tie up the dinghy. "All the stores are right around there," he said as he cast off the dinghy painter for her.

The Straw Market seemed a good place to start and Lisa quickly spotted the open-air shed. Six native women chatted as they wove dried palm fronds into a variety of articles. Lisa wandered among the displays of dolls, hats, purses, belts and finally had to buy a huge straw tote bag to hold all her purchases.

The Ebb Tide gift shop offered the works of Bahamian artists and craftsmen. She bought a pair of batik shorts in varying shades of blue and a long-sleeved batiste shirt in pale blue.

The clerk told her the dyes used in the coloring process were all made from native berries and seeds. Among the many items on display Lisa discovered a small oil painting that she just had to have. It was of a narrow Hope Town street—its colorful houses huddled together, separated only by the brilliant foliage of native shrubs and flowers and casuarinas. The picture showed the harbor and lighthouse in the background.

"You can see that actual scene if you don't mind a short walk," the shopkeeper told her.

On her way to the top of the hill, Lisa stopped at a grocery store and bought a hand of green bananas. We'll hang them on the boom to ripen, she decided, as in one of the paintings she'd just seen.

At the top of the small hill, there it was, the exact scene in her new picture. She spotted *Dream Weaver* in the distance. She looked as tiny as the boats in the painting. Then Lisa noticed a larger boat further down the harbor. Even at a distance, she recognized *Happy Daze*.

"You had two phone calls while you were gone," Michael told her as he tied up the dinghy and helped unload her packages.

"Phone calls? What're you talking about."

"Well, CB calls. The eye doc said your contacts were a standard prescription and he would pick them up at the Marsh Harbour airport tonight. Pop told him you'd be at the clinic tomorrow morning."

"Hey, super! And who else called?"

"*Happy Daze* is here."

"So what?"

"Jessica's having a dinner party—she wants you and me to come over and barbeque with them tonight."

"You've got to be kidding! *Jessica* asked *me* to a party?"

"Uh, it was David who asked. He said Jessica's feeling sorry about the feud and he thinks she wants to make up with you."

"I don't believe it, Michael."

"Believe it . . . I told him we'd come."

"Thanks, but no thanks."

"Aw, c'mon, Lisa, maybe she really is sorry. The least you could do is give her a chance to show it."

"No way! I told you before! I don't want to even be around her."

"Listen, Lisa, I know you don't think much of the way she looks and acts, but you've got to accept people the way they are. There must be something good in Jessica, something you'd like about her if you'd just look for it."

"Don't lecture me, Michael. I don't have to accept Jessica at all. All I have to do is stay away from her. I'll never see her again after this week, so what difference does it make, anyhow?"

"This is silly, Lisa. I'll be there. And with David, Cindy and Peter around you won't have to do more than be polite to Jessica."

"I'm not going! But you go, Michael, if you think she's so great."

"Okay, I will. If you change your mind— they're wearing shorts and the dinghy leaves *Dream Weaver* at seven."

Lisa stomped off to her cabin. What a mess, she thought. If she went, she'd risk another confrontation with Jessica. If she didn't go, she'd risk Jessica's further flirtation with Michael.

Deep, deep in her heart Lisa knew that Michael wasn't hers for keeps. But for just a little while longer, she told herself, she wanted to pretend that she'd have him forever.

"Lisa, I'm going ashore to the post office," Michael called to her. "Do you need anything?"

"Nope. I've already bought out the town."

"Have you made up your mind about the party?"

"Yes . . . yes, I have—I guess I'll go."

Jessica and her friends helped Michael and Lisa tie up their dinghy and climb the ladder to *Happy Daze*' deck.

"Nice of you to come," Jessica said to Lisa. "Your shorts are great. Did you get them here?"

The unusual warmth in Jessica's voice made Lisa apprehensive. Just what was she up to now? David offered to give Lisa a tour of the boat.

"Where're Jessica's aunt and uncle?" Lisa asked David as they went down below to admire the spacious quarters.

"Visiting friends in Marsh Harbour—they'll bring 'em back later."

She wished they were aboard now. She knew her mom always insisted that a chaperone be present at the parties Lisa attended. And that wasn't always so awful, Lisa thought, as she remembered some of the escapades of her schoolmates. Now, here she was in enemy territory, and she didn't know how or when Jessica would attack.

"Gee, I thought *Dream Weaver* was something, but this boat is like a floating condominium," Lisa said to David.

"Yeah, they've got a washer and dryer, dishwasher, trash compactor—all the comforts of home. There are stereo speakers all over the place."

"I hear 'em loud and clear." Lisa tried to keep up her end of the conversation with David, but she also had to keep an eye on Jessica and Michael as they danced in the carpeted salon. Jessica's other friends, Cindy and Peter, were in the cockpit broiling chicken over charcoal embers. Fumes of spicy barbecue sauce filled the boat.

As Lisa plotted how to sit with Michael at the elaborately set table, she noticed Jessica putting placecards at each seat.

"We're going to eat soon," Jessica said. "David, will you give me a hand with the salad?"

After they had disappeared into the cavernous galley, Lisa studied the nautical-looking table. White plastic plates were decorated with red anchors in the center and rimmed in a blue rope pattern, heavy plastic glasses bore the same design. Large red, white and blue paper napkins were imprinted with *"Happy Daze"* and the placecards matched the napkins.

Lisa glanced around furtively. By squinting, she could just make out that Michael and

Jessica were to sit next to each other. She reached for the offending cards.

"What're you doing, Lisa?" demanded Jessica, suddenly appearing behind her.

"Oh—um . . . I knew you probably forgot that the hostess should sit at the end of the table so I was just fixing up the cards for you."

"Don't you dare—"

Michael interrupted the impending argument. "Hey, you two, knock it off. Anyhow, who wants to eat down here when we can sit on deck and watch the sunset."

He scooped up two place settings and thrust one at Lisa. He heaped some salad on his plate, took a glass of iced tea and indicated to Lisa that she do the same.

A reddish glow from the blazing tropical sunset washed over the harbor and the hillside homes. The ruffled tempers were forgotten as they gorged on the scrumptious meal.

Soon, the moon—an orange ball of fire—rose above the horizon. The group, awed by the splendor of the night, chatted quietly and amicably.

That's because Jessica isn't here, Lisa thought to herself. She hoped it would take Jessica forever to clean up the galley. What makes a girl like Jessica tick? she wondered. Michael had once said Jessica needed to be the center of attention and would do anything to get there. Just tonight Michael had said there was something good in Jessica, something Lisa would like if she just looked for it. What is good about Jessica? Lisa asked herself. Her voluptuous figure, long blonde hair, sexy clothes. No, Lisa reasoned, Michael meant a different kind of goodness, an inner good. Well, if it were there it must be deeply buried, Lisa decided. However, she guessed she'd better do as Michael had suggested— accept Jessica as she was. After all, she would only have to see her for one more week.

10

"Can we show Lisa the castle?" Michael asked his pop.

"Might as well. It's only a few miles out of the way and we'll get to Marsh Harbour before the chickens are awake, anyhow," said the sleepy Skipper.

"What's the castle?" Lisa asked. She didn't feel at all guilty at having roused everyone at dawn to start the short trip to Marsh Harbour. After all, today was the day she'd get her contacts!

"It's straight out of a fairy tale—a real castle plunked on a hill at Sugarloaf Cay," Michael told her.

"I see it already," cried Lisa as the Skipper

slowly and cautiously guided *Dream Weaver* through a narrow channel.

Lisa snapped a picture of the castle's largest turret. Her fertile imagination pictured Juliet standing there, leaning over the parapet and wanting to jump over the low wall into Romeo's arms.

"Does someone live there? Who built it?"

"I don't know if anyone still lives there," Michael said. "The guy who built it was Doctor Cottman—a medic who sailed around these parts giving health care to the poor."

"Wow, what a guy. Why'd he build this place?"

"You can find out all about it in his book, *Out Island Doctor*. It's kind of out-of-date now, but it's a great story about the customs and lives of the Bahamian people."

"Wait'll I write that down. What'd you say his name was?"

"Cottman—can't think of his first name."

"Evans," offered the Skipper.

"Gee, thanks for bringing me here, Skipper. I'll get the book as soon as I get home." The thought of going home and leaving Michael momentarily clouded the brightness of Lisa's day. She sighed as she rolled down the sleeves of Michael's shirt to protect her arms from the burning morning sun.

"How'd they get here before us?" Lisa pointed to *Happy Daze* already at anchor in the crowded harbor.

"Didn't go to see the castle, I guess," said Michael.

As the men scanned the water for a good anchorage, Lisa admired the sumptuous homes on the shore side of Marsh Harbour. Flowering trees—red, yellow and purple— cascaded down the hills of what was called, according to Michael, Pelican Shore.

"Lisa, are you ready to go for your contacts?" asked her dad. "I'll go with you—I have to be there to write a check, anyhow."

After tying up the dinghy at the high concrete Union Jack pier, they climbed slick, steep rock steps to the flat surface of the dock. A young boy offered to watch their boat. "Not really necessary," her dad said, "but that's how these kids make a living."

Lisa pulled her dad along to the clinic where Doctor Jones waited for them. In seconds the flimsy soft contacts were in place on Lisa's eyeballs. The doc warned her that contacts would make her eyes more sensitive to the sun so she selected a pair of oversized stylish sunglasses with dark green lenses. "Come back around lunch time and I'll check you again," she was told.

"Listen, Lisa, I've got to get back to the boat and finish up some paperwork," her dad said as they left the clinic. "It's something I want you to mail for me from the Boston airport—that way I'm sure it'll get where it's going. So I'll take the dink," he continued, "and you can call on the Union Jack Hotel's CB when you're ready to come back to the boat. Or you can find a kid at the dock who has a boat and give him fifty cents to run you out to *Dream Weaver*."

"Okay. I want to buy some presents anyhow. So I'll shop until I gotta go back to the doc's."

"Why don't you buy your mother a nice present?" her dad suggested as he gave her a wad of American dollars mixed with the more colorful Bahamian bills. Lisa found it interesting the way she could use both kinds of currency interchangeably.

Marsh Harbour's shopping district didn't have the charm Lisa had admired in the settlements she'd visited. The town bustled—there were paved streets, cars and taxis, along with the motorcycles and bikes she'd seen everywhere. She noticed only one traffic light as she browsed among the busy streets. A tall, erect policeman stood in front of Barclay's Bank, resplendent in his black, red and gold militarylike uniform with a helmet to protect him from the blazing sun.

Even wearing her sunglasses, Lisa squinted

in the bright light so she purchased a huge floppy straw hat in a small souvenir shop. This wasn't the sort of place to look for her mom's present, so Lisa strolled further up the street until she found the Loyalist Shoppe. There she found the perfect present for her mom—a string of smoothly rounded pink coral beads. Should she get the matching earrings? Lisa wondered. Her mom never wore them, but maybe she'd primp a little more now that she was getting married. Lisa bought the earrings.

Back at the medical clinic, Dr. Jones handed her a pair of glasses similar to those she'd lost.

"Your dad wanted to surprise you with these," he said.

"But why do I need 'em now that I have contacts?"

"After the novelty wears off you'll have days when you don't want to bother with your contacts. And you shouldn't wear them swimming or on a really windy day."

"I'll never wear glasses again!" she exclaimed. She was amazed at how clearly she could see, even read, with the little soft circles, like Saran Wrap, in her eyes,

"Well, you're going to wear them right now. You've had your contacts on long enough for the first day. You can add a couple of hours a day and by the end of a week you'll be wearing them full time—except when you go to bed, of course."

After a short lesson in inserting and removing the lenses and learning the necessary daily care, Lisa left the clinic and walked toward the pier and a ride back to *Dream Weaver*. She'd walked so much her ankle ached and she yearned for her cane.

She considered lunching in Union Jack's restaurant, but she decided she was too excited and tired to eat. She plunked herself on a bench in a small park near the restaurant and looked out idly at the dock. In a flash, she recognized two figures, their arms around each other. Jessica and Michael! They had just exchanged an affectionate kiss. Stunned, Lisa watched as, holding hands, they descended the stone steps, got into Jessica's motorboat and roared off to *Dream Weaver* where Jessica let Michael off. She blew him a good-bye kiss and went to *Happy Daze*.

Lisa stood immobilized and incredulous. She was so numb with anger and amazement that she didn't notice The Fathers dinking toward her to the dock.

"You okay, Lisa?" her dad asked.

"Oh, sure, just tired from too much walking."

"Too tired to row the dinghy back to the boat?"

"I guess not."

"We're going to the airport for your tickets. Then do some business at a couple of banks," her dad told her.

"Michael's aboard and waiting to tell you something important," the Skipper said. "See you later, Lisa."

He's in love with Jessica, Lisa thought. Why else would he kiss her like that? She was determined not to show him how much she cared. Her greeting was cool as Michael helped her from the dinghy to *Dream Weaver*.

"Wow, am I glad to see you! Wait'll you hear my news."

"Oh, I just can't wait, Michael," she said sarcastically.

"What's the matter? You mad at me?"

"Of course I'm not mad at you. I know you couldn't help it if Jessica grabbed you and kissed you and forced you to put your arms around her. I saw the whole love scene on the dock."

"For heaven's sake, Lisa, you don't understand. Just let me tell you what happened!"

"Please, spare me the details."

"The details aren't what you think."

"Worse, maybe?"

Against her will her eyes filled with tears of hurt. Her glasses got all steamy and she took them off and looked at him mistily.

"Okay, go ahead and tell me if it's so important to you."

"Okay," he said. "Just calm down. Sit here and listen."

She sat stiffly next to him on the couch.

"After you left to get your contacts Jessica came over to our boat—"

"Just get on with it, Michael. Tell me why you kissed her."

"—and since you weren't here she had a Coke with The Fathers and me."

"That sounds cozy. So why the kiss?"

"It's a long story. Will you be quiet and let me tell it."

"Sorry, go ahead."

"She wanted to talk to you. She said she wanted to apologize. My pop said that he didn't think that was too bad an idea. He added that he thought the trick that she had pulled with our dinghy was more dangerous than funny, and that he felt strongly about harbor pollution. Then your dad got into it and said she owed you an apology for calling you a thief. She started to cry and your dad got embarrassed and said, "Well, Miss . . . Miss whatever your name is—"

Lisa looked up sharply. "That's funny, Michael. We never really did hear her last name. The first time we saw her she said something like: 'I'm Jessica and these are my friends Cindy and David and Peter—and Aunt Anita and Uncle Ed.' None of us ever got formally introduced. Oh, how I wish I'd never even met her."

"Wait'll you hear the rest of the story. It's incredible! Jessica told The Fathers: 'I'm Jessica Lynn Eastman from Atlanta.' Lisa, when my pop heard her say that his face went white under his tan."

"Why? What did it mean to him?"

"A lot! Pop said to her: 'Eastman? Eastman? Is your mother's name Margaret?' Jessica told him yes, her mother's name was Margaret, Margaret Eastman."

"I don't understand," Lisa said. "What was your pop talking about? Why was he so upset? What was my dad doing during all this?"

"He was just sitting there staring at Jessica. I warned you this was unbelievable," Michael said. "Remember when I first met you I told you I couldn't even remember my mother's married name, only that she lived somewhere in the south?"

Lisa nodded uncomprehendingly.

"Well, it hit me the same time it hit my

pop—my mother's married name is Eastman, Margaret Eastman, and she lives in Atlanta, Georgia! Jessica is her daughter—Jessica is my half sister!"

Lisa was speechless. Michael's *half sister*, she thought. Not his girl friend.

"It's like a soap opera," she said. "Quick, Michael, what happened next?"

"Not much. Pop made some nasty comment about Jessica being the kind of daughter he'd expect his ex-wife to have. That made Jessica cry even harder."

"Go on, go on," Lisa urged.

"Your dad said he knew you'd appreciate an apology from her. She seemed weepy and upset, and I felt sorry for her so I took her ashore to Union Jack's for lunch. We talked for hours. You saw us while we were waiting for a boy to bring Jessica's boat around."

"What I saw didn't look like a halfbrotherly kiss!"

"Aw, c'mon, Lisa, lay off that stuff. It was a real shock for both of us."

"Gee, the whole thing seems hard to believe!"

"Well, you know the old saying about truth being stranger than fiction."

"Did she tell you anything about her mother —I mean, your mother?"

"Yeah, and she sounds like a neat person.

I'm gonna try to meet her before I go to college in September."

"But what about your pop?"

"I'd hate to do it behind pop's back, I sure don't want to hurt him. But I just have to get to know my own mother. I always planned to do it sometime—when I wasn't living with pop anymore. But now that I've met Jessica, well—"

"Did she tell you why the Skipper hates your mother so much?"

"Nope, she doesn't have a clue. Her mother—wow, *my* mother—never mentioned her first marriage. Jessica didn't even know she had a half brother somewhere in the world."

"I wonder, does she look like her mother? She sure doesn't look like you."

"She showed me a picture of her—our—mother, she's a pretty blonde—Jessica and I both have her hair. But Jessica says she looks just like her dad. And, I forgot—her dad has a son from his first marriage, he's a year older than Jessica. Her dad's first wife died when that son was born. So I guess now I have a step–half brother, or whatever you'd call him."

"How about Jessica's aunt and uncle? How come they didn't recognize your pop's name when he talked to them about Jessica?"

"They're related to Jessica on her father's

side. Like I said, Margaret Eastman clammed up about her past, so the aunt and uncle probably never even heard the name Montgomery."

"Boy," said Lisa, "My mom keeps telling me I should be a writer. All this would make a great story!"

"Yeah. And with your imagination you could probably figure out why my pop hated my mom so much that he wouldn't even let her see me after I was six or seven."

"She must have done something really awful to him."

"Yeah, and I'm not so sure I want to find out about it before I meet her. It might prejudice me against her before I even meet her."

Lisa fixed iced tea and they moved to the shade-covered cockpit. Both watched *Happy Daze* as she swung on her anchor.

"Lisa, will you do me a big favor?" Michael asked.

"Sure."

"Just talk to Jessica, give her a chance to apologize to you. When she tells you something about herself, you'll understand her better. Our fathers will be best friends forever so you and I will always be friends through them. Now that I have a sister it would make me happy to know that she was your friend, too."

Lisa's sigh was resigned. "I guess that makes sense."

"Anyhow," Michael went on, "you should do it for your own sake. You said you'd never forget this wonderful trip. That means you'll never forget the un-wonderful parts of it, either. If you don't talk it out with Jessica now, you'll always wonder why she acted that way. Please do it, Lisa."

"Okay, I'll try."

"Thanks, you're a super friend." He hugged her. It was a hug of gratitude, not affection. "Jessica's alone on the boat—all the others have gone ashore to shop. Can I dink you over there right now?"

She tied Michael's precious shirt around her neck for moral support. "Okay," she sighed, "let's go."

11

A red-eyed, tear-stained Jessica helped Lisa aboard *Happy Daze*.

"Oh, Lisa, thank you for coming." She put her arms around Lisa and wept into her long hair. "Let's go to my cabin—I need some more Kleenex."

"Jessica," said Lisa, "this isn't necessary, you know. I honestly don't want to make a big deal out of it." The two girls sat on a large double bed with Lisa as far away from Jessica as she could get.

"Lisa, you've gotta let me talk to you. I'm all shook up and maybe I won't make much sense. But I've gotta tell you how sorry I am about the awful things I did."

"Okay. I accept your apology. Is that all?" Lisa said stiffly.

"Please don't be like that. Please listen to me because you've got to understand why I did all that."

"I'll try, Jessica."

"I don't know how to say this . . . it was . . . it was because I was jealous of you."

"Wha-a-t?"

"Yes. Girls like you are so . . . so nice . . . so normal. The first time I saw you I envied you. You're exactly what I think a girl should be—slim figure, neat clothes. You sounded so smart—"

"I don't understand—"

"I got mad because Michael liked you so much. And David was always telling me how great you were. They're the kind of boys I want to know—but I always get stuck with kids like Peter."

"Peter? What's the matter with him?"

"He's just like all the other boys I know—fast—fresh—"

"Hey, Jessica, with your looks you could get any boy you wanted!"

"My looks, ha ha! They're the problem. I've been busty since I was twelve, my hair looks bleached and it isn't, I diet all the time but I'm still fat."

"You're not *fat*, Jessica."

"No, 'voluptuous' is what they call it. I'm a voluptuous, dumb blonde—that's supposed to be sexy. So all the sexy boys chase me and the nice ones go around with girls like you. Girls like you don't ever like me—Cindy's my only friend, and I don't know how she stands me. So I go with a gang of kids I don't even like—kids who think I'm something I'm not."

"Your clothes have a lot to do with that, Jessica."

"Yeah, I know. I guess I decided if everyone thought I *was* a sexy fox, I might as well look like one. I bought most of that stuff after I got to Florida, just for this trip. My mom would die if she ever saw me in those bikinis. At least they got me a lot of attention."

"Why is attention so important to you, Jessica?"

"I guess it's because I think I have to *make* people like me. I don't think I have much to offer the world—I'm not very smart, and I don't read much, I hate sports—"

"Seems to me that you don't think very much of yourself."

"I hate myself! And when I hear girls like you talking to guys like David and Michael about books and things—then I hate you. So I have to get back at you."

"That's awful, Jessica. How can you expect anyone to like you if you don't like yourself?"

"I'm so ashamed of the things I did just to get Michael and David to pay attention to me. You know, I never had a drink in my life, but Peter talked me into it. I should have said no, the way David did. Man, was I sick afterward —and scared about what could have happened to me.

"Listen, Jessica, I didn't mean to sound like the goody-goody you accused me of being—"

"Lisa, please try and forget how awful I was to you."

By now the two girls were close together on the big bed, sharing the box of tissues.

"It's okay, Jessica. I'm beginning to understand." Lisa enfolded the sobbing older girl in her arms and smoothed her blonde hair.

"I read in Ann Landers that kids who have to do what everybody else does—peer pressure, it's called—anyhow, kids do this because they don't like themselves, the column said."

"Gee, that's heavy, but I know what you mean. I've made such a mess of my life already—even my mom and daddy have given up on me. What can I do to like myself more?"

"Be your own woman—keep your head on straight and your standards high, no matter what the other kids do. Change your image!"

"Gee, Lisa, how can I change my image?"

"Well, you could start by changing your

looks. Cut your hair short. If you have less blonde hair it won't look so fake."

"Yeah, I guess you're right. And I use too much makeup on purpose, too. My mom is always after me to tone it down, and the nail polish and—"

"Oh, who listens to mothers," said Lisa. She knew she'd listened too much, which was as bad as not listening at all. Wow, thought Lisa, who's figuring herself out here—Jessica or Lisa?

"And you can change the way you dress."

"I guess I could do that—after I lose some weight. I guess I could do that, too—I nibble a lot because I'm so bored and unhappy."

"Okay," said Lisa. "Now that you've changed your looks the next thing to do is change your friends."

"That'd be kind of hard my last year in high school."

"Well, just don't run around with the same crowd so much. Study, read, do volunteer work—you could be a Red Cross Candy Striper in a hospital this summer. You'd meet lots of new girls that way—and they'll know different boys. You can always meet kids in church, too."

"Hey, that's a great idea. My crowd never goes to church and my mom and daddy are always after me to go. And, ya know, I was planning to go to the same college as the rest of my crowd. Maybe I should go somewhere else where no one knows me. My step-brother goes to the University of North Carolina, maybe I could go there."

"Or to FSU where Michael will be," Lisa said ruefully. Her face wore a wistful expression.

"Lisa, are you in love with Michael?"

"Oh, Jessica! It's so awful! I like him so much. I can't stand the thought of not being with Michael."

Now it was Jessica who comforted Lisa and handed her fresh Kleenex.

"You'll get over it, Lisa. It'll take time, but you will. Michael says you've changed a lot in the few weeks he's known you. Your life will be different when you get home, you'll see. Anyhow, he'll always be your friend—and girls our age need a *friend* more than we need a serious boyfriend." Jessica hugged her reassuringly.

Lisa wiped her eyes and blew her nose just in time—Michael was in the dinghy calling out that he'd come to pick her up.

"Did it go okay?" he asked as he rowed her back to *Dream Weaver*.

"Great. I'll tell you about it later. Right now

175

I'm beat and can hardly wait to get back to *Dream Weaver* and take a nap."

As Lisa awoke from a refreshing late afternoon nap she heard The Fathers and Michael puttering around the galley. They're fixing dinner, she thought. Since this would be their last real meal together on *Dream Weaver*, Lisa dressed up for the occasion.

"Michael," she called out, "I'm going to wear my contacts for a few hours. Would you come and see if I put them in okay?"

"Hey, you did great," he said as he stood behind her cabin desk and watched her place the delicate lenses in her eyes.

"As well as Christine?"

"Better! She doesn't have to worry about bumping into long eyelashes."

Laughing together, they went to the dinette where The Fathers had set out a microwaved gourmet meal.

Lisa sensed a strained atmosphere—even the Skipper was subdued. She wondered if it was because everyone else realized this was their last dinner. No, there was more to it than that, she decided. After all, *she* was the only one who had anything to be sad about. She'd be leaving Michael; the rest of them would only be leaving each other.

"Michael," his pop said, "this business with

Jessica has made me decide to tell you something I'd rather not talk about."

Lisa's dad started to leave the table and take her with him.

"No, old buddy," the Skipper said, "you already know the whole story. And Michael will tell Lisa, anyhow. So I'll just say what I have to say as fast as I can and I don't ever want to talk about it again. Understood, Michael?"

"Understood, Pop."

"John here," the Skipper pointed to Lisa's dad, "and I were best friends all through Yale Law School. We had another close friend, Paul Eastman. In our last year, Paul got engaged to a girl named Margaret. They planned to get married as soon as Paul got his degree. But then he decided he didn't want to be a lawyer and he didn't want to rush into marriage until he got into some other line of work. So Margaret broke their engagement."

Lisa gasped. Her dad gave her a warning look.

"Anyhow," the Skipper continued. "I was with a law firm in Boston. That's where Margaret lived. I started seeing a lot of her, and eventually we got married. The only good thing about our marriage was the birth of Michael. Soon after he was born, Margaret and I went to my class reunion. Paul Eastman was at the reunion too. He had been married, but his wife died when their son was born. We all felt sorry for him—especially Margaret."

Lisa sneaked a look at Michael. He was staring at his pop with an expressionless face.

"Right after that I had to go to Saudi Arabia on business," the Skipper went on. "I had hardly gotten there when Margaret wrote a letter telling me that our marriage was a mistake and she wanted a divorce. She said she had always loved Paul Eastman and still loved him and she wanted to marry him as soon as she could. So I flew home and we got divorced. Later I heard that Margaret and John Eastman had a baby, and, as we found out today, the baby turned out to be Jessica."

Just as Lisa was about to say something her dad gently kicked at her under the table. And right on her bad ankle, too.

"I got full custody of Michael," the Skipper continued. "I wanted to change my life completely so I moved to Fort Lauderdale and opened my own law firm. A couple of times a year I'd take Michael to Miami and his mother would fly down from Atlanta and spend the weekend in a hotel with him. When he was six, maybe seven, he started asking questions about his mother. And I—well, to be honest, his mother and I decided it was a tough situation for a kid to accept. She had Jessica and also Paul Eastman's son to raise and she didn't want them to be confused, either. And I wasn't about to let her have Michael. We decided it would be best if she stayed out of Michael's life until he, and the other children, were old enough to accept, or at least understand, the whole story."

Michael started to interrupt, but his pop stopped him.

"Wait a minute, Michael, I'm almost finished. I was going to tell you all about it this summer, but bumping into Jessica took care of that. I realize now I should have told you a couple of years ago—"

"A couple of years ago I wouldn't have understood, Pop," Michael said.

"Maybe not. Anyhow, now that you know I hope you'll see your mother and get to know her. I hope what I've told you won't prejudice you against her. I don't want you to judge her at all. Leaving me for someone else wasn't all that bad. I think it was the blow to my ego that's made me so bitter about her all these years—"

"Hey, Pop, that's enough," Michael said. "Like you said, you'd tell it and you never wanted to talk about it again. So let's drop it right now. Just one more thing," Michael got up from the table and hugged the Skipper with a huge bear hug, "you're the greatest father and mother a guy ever had."

Lisa held her dad's hand so hard that the circulation in her arm almost stopped.

"Let's clean up this mess then go sit outside," said Lisa.

"You and Michael have got galley duty," the Skipper said. "And how about bringing your fathers some coffee before you get to work?"

While they tidied the galley, Lisa told Michael about most of her talk with Jessica. He thanked her for helping his half sister, but he didn't seem to want to talk about it.

"What d'ya think of the mess about my mother?" he asked.

"Like I said before, it's a soap opera, a real sudsy one."

"At least you know how to end your book!"

"Yeah, I'll have to get a notebook and write it all down so I won't forget anything. Michael, you're not shook up from hearing about your mother, are you?"

"Nah, not really. I'm kinda numb, though. A lot has hit me all in one day—a sister, a brother, a mother—"

"You forgot your step-father."

"I'm like you, Lisa—I don't need a step-father because I've got a perfectly super father right here."

12

"**P**ut all the stuff you bought in your big straw bag, Lisa; you might need to show it at Miami customs," Michael told her.

Her dad and the Skipper gulped their morning coffee while Lisa and Michael breakfasted on their usual peanut butter concoctions.

"You'd be smart to make a list of your purchases—gifts you gave or received don't count—then maybe customs won't ransack your luggage," the Skipper advised.

"That's a good idea, Lisa," her dad added. "And you might as well give me any Bahamian money you have left so I'll have something to spend on the trip home."

"But it's so beautiful! I wanted to keep it." She reached for her wallet. "Look at this dollar bill—it's every color of the rainbow, and when you hold it up to the light you can see a large conch."

"Let's see those coins," said Michael. He picked through the pile Lisa handed him. "Can I have this one for a lucky piece?" It was a twenty-five cent piece engraved with a Bahamian sailing sloop.

"Sure," said Lisa, "and I'll keep one, too. And this penny with a starfish. And look at the rest of the change—here's a pineapple, a bonefish, a hibiscus—geez, aren't they neat!"

"Speaking of change, Lisa," her dad said— and quite sternly, Lisa thought. "The biggest change your mother will notice in you is the slang you've picked up—the 'ya knows, geez, yeahs' you've added to your vocabulary. You don't sound like you and she won't like that. I'm not sure I do."

"Yeah, you're right. I'm gonna do somethin' about it soon, ya know?"

Michael joined in the laughter and said: "She caught that from me, I guess. I promise I'll teach her to speak English again on the trip home."

"At least I learned that you don't say 'y'all' to one person." Lisa looked at Michael impishly and they giggled as they remembered Jessica's exaggerated southern drawl.

Lisa realized she was laughing with tears in her eyes. She watched Michael stuff the dinghy with their luggage, then all four of them crammed into the remaining space. She didn't even have enough elbow room to get her camera from her straw bag to take one last picture of *Dream Weaver* at anchor in the harbor.

"I'll be at the Conch Inn for dinner tonight, Lisa. Will you call me about nine so I'll know you got home all right?" asked her dad. He reached across the crowded taxi that was taking them to the airport and gave her a card with the Inn's number.

"Okay, *Mother*," she said with a twinkle in her loving look at him. "Hey, look who's here," she said as they all spilled out of the cab at the airport terminal.

David and a pretty blonde girl ran toward them. It was Jessica! A flattering golden helmet of hair framed her face, pale eye shadow highlighted sky-blue eyes, soft coral-tinted lips outlined straight white teeth, the same coral glistened on fingers and toes. The navy-blue boy-type shirt worn outside of her jeans gave her a natural, sporty look.

"I just had to come and say good-bye," she

said as she hugged Lisa. "I hope y'all don't mind," Jessica said to Lisa's dad and the Skipper. Lisa wasn't certain The Fathers even recognized the transformed girl.

"How d'ya like my hair? Cindy cut it," said Jessica, head held high, with poise and confidence.

"You look neat," Lisa said as she squeezed Jessica's hand.

"Yeah, Sis, you'll be okay," said Michael. "C'mon, Lisa, The Fathers are frantic, we haven't got much time to check in and board our plane."

"Lisa," David called after her, "maybe I'll give you a call when I get to Yale."

"That'll be great," she yelled as Michael pulled her to the ticket counter.

"D'ya think he'll really call you?" Michael asked as they stood on the check-in line.

"How could he? He doesn't even know my last name—and I don't know his," she laughed. "Anyhow, it'll be fun to tell my best friend a Yalie might call me—not that mom would let me date anyone in college."

"Then she wouldn't let you date me?"

"Oh, that'd be different. You're a friend, not a date." She smiled wistfully at Michael.

There were no prolonged farewells with The Fathers. After a few hugs and kisses Michael and Lisa were seatbelted and airborne.

"Gee, my mom will die when she sees her little girl in this outfit," Lisa said as she carefully wiped a dribble of iced tea from her pink designer jeans.

"I don't think it'll take her long to realize you're not a little girl any longer. You have to stand up for who you want to be—then she'll treat you like the young woman you've become."

"I sure feel like I've discovered a whole new person!"

"Just keep acting like one, Lisa. Then your mom'll see that you're an individual and not her clone. She'll establish a whole new relationship with you—like you and your dad."

"Yeah, and I'll have to get used to her being different, too—especially since she's marrying Barney—Professor Barnett. Ya know, all the kids like him, he's really with it. I bet he'll tell her I could be a computer engineer if I wanted to."

"Geez, Lisa, with your looks and personality —and certainly your brains—you can do anything you make up your mind to do. You need a dream that's all your own, something that really matters to you—"

A devastated, lonely feeling swept through Lisa's young body. How, she wondered, could she leave this considerate, understanding boy.

"Oh, Michael, you're all that matters to me right now." Tears streamed down her face.

"Don't you ever say that to anyone, Lisa! Not to a friend or your parents or even a husband if ya get married. You've got to have your own identity and not depend on any one else for your happiness."

Michael's hand was tight and warm in hers. She looked at his tanned left hand covering hers and remembered something important.

"Did your pop ever give you back your ring, Michael?"

"Yeah, he did—right after I shot the shark that chased you."

"Why aren't you wearing it?"

"I've put it on a couple of times, but it reminds me too much of what I did to you."

"But that's all over now."

"Well, it was an awful experience! I learned a lot from it, but I don't want to be reminded of it every time I see the ring—I just can't wear it—so I want you to have it, Lisa."

"Oh, no, Michael, I can't wear your class ring! That would mean we were going steady or that we were in love."

He opened a small white velvet box and Lisa gasped when she saw that the dazzling sapphire from his ring had been set into a pendant. The sparkling gem nestled in a narrow gold rim and hung from a short thin gold chain.

Lisa lifted her heavy hair as Michael clasped the jewel around her neck.

"Thank you." That was all she trusted herself to say.

The short flight to Miami ended. Lisa and Michael picked up their baggage, went through customs and had to sprint across the big terminal to get Lisa aboard her plane to Boston.

"Bye, Lisa, it's been great."

"Bye, Michael—I'll think of you everytime I lose a contact."

The big plane—and Michael—receded into the distance.

Lisa forced back tears. She told herself she couldn't waste any time crying over past experiences—when there were a million more to come. Wow, she thought, that's something Michael might have said.

She caressed the lovely pendant and was grateful for Michael's influence on her life.

She looked down at the gold pine cone pin and recognized how much her dad had contributed to her new maturity.

The plane's cabin was too warm and Lisa slipped off the jacket the Skipper had given her. She folded it neatly in her lap. She studied the blue embroidered words: *Dream Weaver*.

Then she realized that those words said it all. She knew that nobody else grew up for her. *She* was the dream weaver—and from now on her life would be wonderful, exciting and magical.

15-Day Free Trial Offer
6 Silhouette Romances

6 Silhouette Romances, free for 15 days! We'll send you 6 new Silhouette Romances to keep for 15 days, absolutely free! If you decide not to keep them, send them back to us. You pay nothing.

Free Home Delivery. But if you enjoy them as much as we think you will, keep them by paying the invoice enclosed with your free trial shipment. We'll pay all shipping and handling charges. You get the convenience of Home Delivery and we pay the postage and handling charge each month.

Don't miss a copy. The Silhouette Book Club is the way to make sure you'll be able to receive every new romance we publish before they're sold out. There is no minimum number of books to buy and you can cancel at any time.

- - - - - **This offer expires May 31, 1984** - - - -

 Silhouette Book Club, Dept. SF1273
120 Brighton Road, Clifton, NJ 07012

Please send me 6 Silhouette Romances to keep for 15 days, absolutely free. I understand I am not obligated to join the Silhouette Book Club unless I decide to keep them.

NAME _____

ADDRESS _____

CITY _____

STATE _____ ZIP _____

First Love from Silhouette

THERE'S NOTHING QUITE AS SPECIAL AS A **FIRST LOVE.**

—— $1.75 each ——

- 2 ☐ GIRL IN THE ROUGH
  Wunsch
- 3 ☐ PLEASE LET ME IN
  Beckman
- 4 ☐ SERENADE
  Marceau
- 6 ☐ KATE HERSELF
  Erskine
- 7 ☐ SONGBIRD
  Enfield
- 14 ☐ PROMISED KISS
  Ladd

- 15 ☐ SUMMER ROMANCE
  Diamond
- 16 ☐ SOMEONE TO LOVE
  Bryan
- 17 ☐ GOLDEN GIRL
  Erskine
- 18 ☐ WE BELONG TOGETHER
  Harper
- 19 ☐ TOMORROW'S WISH
  Ryan
- 20 ☐ SAY PLEASE!
  Francis

—— $1.95 each ——

- 24 ☐ DREAM LOVER
  Treadwell
- 26 ☐ A TIME FOR US
  Ryan
- 27 ☐ A SECRET PLACE
  Francis
- 29 ☐ FOR THE LOVE OF LORI
  Ladd
- 30 ☐ A BOY TO DREAM ABOUT
  Quinn
- 31 ☐ THE FIRST ACT
  London
- 32 ☐ DARE TO LOVE
  Bush
- 33 ☐ YOU AND ME
  Johnson
- 34 ☐ THE PERFECT FIGURE
  March
- 35 ☐ PEOPLE LIKE US
  Haynes

- 36 ☐ ONE ON ONE
  Ketter
- 37 ☐ LOVE NOTE
  Howell
- 38 ☐ ALL-AMERICAN GIRL
  Payton
- 39 ☐ BE MY VALENTINE
  Harper
- 40 ☐ MY LUCKY STAR
  Cassiday
- 41 ☐ JUST FRIENDS
  Francis
- 42 ☐ PROMISES TO COME
  Dellin
- 43 ☐ A KNIGHT TO REMEMBER
  Martin
- 44 ☐ SOMEONE LIKE JEREMY VAUGHN
  Alexander

First Love from Silhouette

Lift Your Spirit This October With
THE MYSTERY KISS
by Elaine Harper

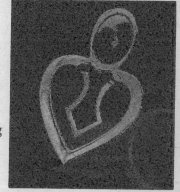